To the Fore with the Tanks!

Percy F. Westerman

To the Fore with the Tanks!

Contact:
BibliotechPress@gmail.com

The present edition is a reproduction of 1917 publication of this work. Minor typographical errors may have been corrected without note, however, for an authentic reading experience the spelling, punctuation, and capitalization have been retained from the original text.

ISBN: 978-1-61895-209-7

CONTENTS

CHAPTER I
TO THE FRONT

"The jolting cattle-trucks pulled up with a disconcerting jerk at the termination of a fifty-mile railway journey, performed in the remarkably record time of fifteen hours.

From a springless truck, on which was painted the legend, "40 hommes ou 8 chevaux," descended fifty-two tired but elated Tommies, thirsty, ravenously hungry, but quite able to keep up a bantering conversation with the peasants who had gathered by the side of the temporary line.

It was a miserable night, even for the Somme district in early March. Rain was falling solidly. The ground was churned into deep mud of the consistency of treacle. The gaunt gables of a dozen roofless houses, silhouetted against the constant glare in the sky, betokened ruined homes and uncomfortable billets; while the loud rumble of distant artillery was in itself ample proof that at last the Second Wheatshires had arrived somewhere on the Western Front—the goal of six months' constant and arduous training.

Into the squelching mud the men stepped blithely. They were used to it by this time. The double line of khaki-clad figures, showing dimly through the darkness, shuffled impatiently. Here and there a man would "hike" his pack to relieve the weight of the webbing equipment over his shoulders, or sling his rifle while he lighted the almost inseparable "fag." The distant flashes of the heavy guns glinted from the wet "tin-hats" of the Tommies, as the unaccustomed head-gear wobbled with every movement of the wearer's head. The issue of steel trench helmets given before the commencement of the railway journey had confirmed the rumour of the past fortnight—that No. 3 Platoon was to be sent to join the rest of the battalion at the Front.

"Ah, well, 'tis certain he hath crossed River Somme,'" quoted Private Graham Alderhame formerly of the Shakesperian Repertoire Company and now a humble foot-slogging Tommy in a noted Line Regiment. "Well, if this is across the Somme I don't think much of it. Another ten miles by motor-bus, I suppose, and then something in the way of grub. Got a cigarette on you, dear boy?"

Private Ralph Setley, who seven months previously had been a bank-clerk in a busy provincial town, placed his rifle against a pile of equipment that was serenely resting in the mud, and fumbled for a packet of smokes. Then, having handed one of the contents to his chum, he struck a match.

The light flickered upon the honest, deeply tanned features of a typical British lad of about nineteen or twenty. In spite of a day of extreme discomfort in the over-crowded horse-box which the French Government placed at the disposal of Allied troops, his eyes twinkled with the excitement of the moment. At last he was within sound of the guns, and more, the chance of meeting a Hun was within measurable distance.

Having lighted Alderhame's cigarette and his own, Setley was about to throw the vilely sulphurous match to the ground when another voice interposed:

"Hold hard, chum. Let's have a light."

Ralph was about to comply with the request when a hand shot out and sent the still flaring match flying through the air.

"What's that for, George?" asked the disappointed applicant for a light, with mingled truculence and resentment.

"'Cause 'tain't for no good; third chap as 'as a light from the same match allus goes West—honest fact," replied Ginger Anderson, a short, wiry man, who, according to his attestation papers, used to be a gamekeeper, although others of his platoon swore that he had been convicted three times for poaching.

"Listen!" exclaimed Alderhame, placing a hand on Setley's shoulder.

A short distance along the double line of waiting Tommies a hungry Kentish man was endeavouring to persuade an ancient paysanne to sell some eggs. Judging by the man's injured tone his efforts were not meeting with success.

"Wot, no compree?" he asked. "Des woffs, des woffs. Blimey, these old Frenchies don't understand their own bloomin' language. Woffs, I said, missis—them wot we calls heggs."

A motor-car with dimmed head-lights dashed up, throwing showers of mud on either side like miniature cascades. From it descended a great-coated staff-officer. The ranks stiffened. Something was in the air. Information, perhaps, as to the place where the tired Tommies were to be billeted.

"Who's in charge of this platoon?" rasped out an authoritative voice.

"I am, sir," replied a subaltern fresh from home, a beardless youth of about nineteen, Stanley Dacres by name. "Details for the Second Wheatshires."

"Quite about time," rejoined the staff officer. "You are to take your men to the reserve trenches. Motor-buses for the first five

2

miles. With luck you ought to be there by midnight. Arms and equipment all correct?"

"All correct, sir."

"Gas masks?"

"Two per man, sir."

"All right; see that one is returned. New pattern gas-helmets will be issued. A guide will accompany you. Good night and good luck."

The staff officer vanished in the darkness, his place being taken by a sergeant who had evidently emerged from an estaminet.

In single file the No. 3 Platoon marched off, ankle deep in liquid mud, the coldness of which penetrated the thick puttees and boots of the men as they made their way towards the supply depot.

The depot was a long, rambling stone building that originally possessed one doorway. Now there were two, a Hun shell having obligingly knocked away twenty or thirty square feet of masonry in the end wall, while of the roof only a few rafters and tiles remained. Tarpaulin sheets had been nailed to the woodwork to form a temporary shelter from the driving rain. The corners of the canvas, flapping in the wind, threatened to demolish the remaining structure, besides allowing a steady stream of water to pour upon the earth and lime-trodden floor.

As each man entered the building he threw one of the two gas-masks in a corner, and in return had a complicated anti-poison-gas device thrust unceremoniously into his hand. Three paces further on he was greeted with half of a very dry loaf and a tin of bully-beef, while as he emerged into the night another gift in the shape of one hundred and fifty rounds of ball ammunition in clips was bestowed on the already heavily weighted Tommy.

"Repairs executed while you wait!" exclaimed Ginger Anderson. "Oh, dash! There goes my bloomin' tucker."

The half-loaf had slipped from his grasp and was rolling in the mud. As he stooped to retrieve it the man next to him cannoned into his unstable form, with the result that Ginger went on all-fours, plus equipment, in the Artois mud.

"Say, sergeant," remarked the luckless private, holding up the bread. "Wot am I ter do wi' this?"

"Get outside it when you're hungry," was the N.C.O.'s unsympathetic reply. "If you've never got to eat stuff worse than that you can thank your lucky stars."

"All aboard for 'Appy 'Ampstead!" shouted a wag as a line of motor-buses, some possessing the original advertisements they had displayed in London Town, snorted up through the blinding rain.

"Silence in the ranks!" ordered the platoon commander.

Even had his order not been given absolute silence fell upon the men as a blinding flash stabbed the darkness, followed by an appalling crash like a concerted roar of a dozen thunder claps. The ground trembled. A partly demolished gable collapsed with a long drawn-out rumble.

"We're under shell fire at last, then," remarked Second-Lieutenant Dacres to the sergeant told off as guide to the platoon.

"Fritz's evening hate, sir," replied the N.C.O. imperturbably. "He drops them occasionally on the high road well behind our lines on the off chance of strafing some of our chaps. That one fell quite five hundred yards away. You'll soon get used to it, sir. There'll be two more coming, and then we can get a move on."

Private Setley could feel his heart beating against his ribs as he waited. Being under shell fire for the first time was decidedly an uncanny sensation. Dimly he wondered if he would ever get used to it.

The second and third projectiles came almost simultaneously, one bursting a quarter of a mile away on the right, the other landing in an already ruined farm building on the outskirts of the village. Beams and masses of brick-bats were tossed sky-high like straws in a gale of wind, while some of the men felt certain that they saw portions of a field gun hurled upwards in the glare of the bursting shell.

"That's the lot," declared the sergeant coolly. "'Tain't like what it used to be. Fritz thinks twice about wasting heavy gun ammunition."

Silently the Tommies boarded the waiting buses. For the time being their natural hilarity was subdued by the unwonted display of war.

"Seeking a bubble reputation at the cannon's mouth,'" declared the ex-actor. "If it weren't for the fact that I've come a very long way to see the fun, I, like Pistol's boy, would give all my fame for a pot of ale and safety. What say you, Setley?"

Private Setley did not reply. Mentally he was comparing his present position with that of a few short months ago. Then he would have given almost anything to be "clear of the Bank." The long hours spent in making up the "half-yearly balance" were loathsome. It was a relief to be able to live an open-air life. Now he was about to realise the dreams of months—yet, somehow, he hardly relished those bursting shells. It was too one-sided to his liking—to be potted at from an unknown distance and be unable to lift so much as a little finger in self-defence.

4

"Wait till it comes to bayonet work," he mused. "Then our fellows will give the Huns a bit of a surprise."

The detachment was really good at bayonet practice. While attached to the Fifth Battalion at home the men had earned unstinted praise from super-critical instructors at the way in which they prodded the suspended sacks.

With a few exceptions all the men of No. 3 Platoon were either Derby men or conscripts. They all had good excuses—or they individually firmly imagined they had—why they should not "join up." It wasn't that they were not patriotic, yet circumstances urged them to hold back as long as possible. They groused while they awaited the long-deferred call. The uncertainty of the whole business was the worst part of it; but when they did join up they made the very best of an unwanted job, went through the training like Trojans, and longed for the order for the Front.

Socially they were a motley lot. In addition to the "former occupations" of men already mentioned there were two solicitors, a 'Varsity graduate, an artist, a general manager, half a score of small business men, several mechanics and labourers and two ex-convicts—all firmly determined to have a slap at Kaiser Bill's grey-coated Huns.

For twenty minutes the line of motor-buses jolted and swayed, sometimes making abrupt turns to avoid deep shell holes, at others slowing down or stopping to allow convoys proceeding in opposite direction to pass. All the while the deafening din continued, increasing in intensity as the distance decreased.

At length the vehicles pulled up at the end of that stage of the journey. The stiff-limbed and sleepy men, hampered by their heavy equipment, got down into the mud once more.

There was very little talking. Every man seemed to be too interested in the novel form of Brock's fireworks to indulge in conversation. As far as the eye could reach the countryside—slightly undulating—was pin-pricked with flashes of gun-fire. Overhead star-shells of varying colours threw a lurid glare upon the mounds of brickwork that at one time formed populous and prosperous villages. Half a mile to the right a church tower still stood, with a jagged hole in one angle. It seemed marvellous that the whole structure had not collapsed. Ahead the road ended abruptly in a mound of earth and stones thrown up by the impact and explosion of a Hun eleven-inch shell. Almost touching the outer edge of the crater was a Calvary—the cross standing out sharply against the artificially lighted horizon. The crucifix was the only object left standing within a radius of a hundred yards from the place where the shell had dropped.

Suddenly a lurid flash, followed almost simultaneously by a roar that outvoiced the distant rumble of the artillery, seemed to burst from the ground within thirty paces of the platoon as they formed up to continue their journey on the march.

The spurt of fire directed upwards at an acute angle was followed by the hideous tearing screech of a huge projectile. A British gun, so cleverly screened that none of the detachment was aware of its existence, had just been fired. "It's only 'Gentle Gerty' saying good night to the Boches, sir," explained the guide. "Now, sir, single file, and no smoking in the ranks."

The Tommies, throwing away their cigarette ends and knocking out their pipes, set out on the last stage of their journey. They were now at the Front.

CHAPTER II
THE COMMUNICATION TRENCH

"For the next fifty yards Private Ralph Setley's range of vision was bounded in front by the steel helmet, bulging pack and hunched shoulders of the man preceding him. Right and left nothing but fields lavishly pitted with shell holes. The only sounds, besides the ever-thunderous roar of the guns, the quelching of the men's boots in the mud.

"Left incline."

The platoon wriggled sideways like an enormous worm. The reason was soon not only apparent to the eye but to the nostrils. A mule, struck down by a shell, was lying half buried in the mud, its legs sticking up grotesquely in the air.

Presently the man preceding Setley seemed to disappear from view. The Tommies in front were descending the steps leading to the long communication trench. For nearly a mile the only way of gaining the reserve and firing trenches was by means of the sunken gallery.

Eight feet down Setley descended. His feet no longer sank to his ankles in mud. The nailed soles of his boots grated upon wire-netting, that, stretched across the seemingly endless line of "duck-boards," prevented the men slipping on the lively pieces of boarding into the slime that formed the major portion of the floor of the trench.

On either hand the stiff, slimy walls of clay, topped by rows of sandbags, threatened to collapse and bury the users of the narrow and tortuous way, for in order to prevent the communicating trench being enfiladed by hostile fire it was a continued succession of twists and turns.

Still the rain poured down remorselessly upon the great-coated Tommies. Here and there portions of the parapet had slipped bodily into the trench, necessitating a tedious clamber over a heap of moist clay of the consistency of soft putty.

Before a hundred yards of the narrow way had been traversed George Anderson, who was immediately in front of Setley, stepped incautiously upon the edge of one of the duck-boards. In a trice the section of woodwork tilted, deporting the man up to his thighs in mud and water, while Ralph, stopping abruptly to avoid the tilted end of the board, was cannoned into by the man behind who happened to be Private Alderhame. The next instant both were sprawling on top of the luckless Anderson, driving his writhing body still deeper into the mud.

With difficulty Ralph and the ex-actor extricated themselves. Ginger was in a worse predicament, for until his comrades gripped his arm and dragged him out by main force he was unable to disengage himself from the clammy embrace of the tenacious clay.

"I came out 'ere for sojering," remarked the aggrieved man. "Not to go in for mudlarkin'. I could get plenty of that at Gravesend."

"Phit! phit!" Something, buzzing like an angry bee, slapped viciously into the mud wall a few inches above Setley's head. Then another, glancing off the steel helmet of the still grumbling Anderson, sent the man staggering into Ralph's arms.

"Keep down as you pass this place," shouted a hoarse voice through the darkness. "The parapet's blown in."

A gap nearly twenty yards in length confirmed the speaker's words. Through this exposed section rifle bullets were whizzing. Apparently the Huns had marked the spot during the hours of daylight and had lashed some rifles to posts, so trained that at fifteen hundred yards they could command this part of the communication trench by night.

The platoon obeyed smartly, yet resentfully. It was bad enough to have to walk through mud. To crawl on one's hands and knees was about the limit.

"Way for the wounded!"

7

The men, most of them still in a prone position, hugged the slippery side of the trench, peering through the darkness at the as yet strange sight.

"Good luck, you blighters!" exclaimed the first of the wounded Tommies, a tall cadaverous man, with his head roughly bandaged and his arm in a sling. "You're going to a hot shop, s'welp me. Fifteen of our chaps copped it in ten minutes. Never mind; it's for Blighty I am."

The next casualty—a man with his left hand blown off at the wrist—was groaning and cursing as he passed, staggering like a drunken man and paying scant heed to the warning to keep well down.

Then two more, borne on stretchers. The knuckles of the bearers rasped the equipment of the Wheatshires, so narrow was the space in which to pass, while in order to cross the "unhealthy" section of the trench the men had to deposit the stretchers on the duck-boards and drag them sleigh fashion.

Three men, hobbling, using their rifles as crutches, completed the pageant of pain.

"Copped it proper," explained one of the wounded. "Never 'ad as much as a blinkin' chance to fire my blessed rifle."

"Wouldn't 'ave been much use if you did, Tommy," rejoined his comrade with a laugh. "You knowed as 'ow you're the rottenest shot in the battalion."

"No need to rub that in afore a lot of strangers," retorted the other. "'Op it; I'll race you to the dressing-station. No more dashed first line trenches for us for a bit, thank 'eaven. Foot it, you blighter, afore your leg gets stiff."

The twain vanished into the darkness, leaving the dank, reeking odours of dirt and sweat in the muggy air.

Another hundred yards and a voice rang out:

"Is that the ration party?"

"No," replied the sergeant. "Reliefs for the Wheatshires."

"Good luck to 'em, then!" rejoined the speaker. "But where the deuce are the rations? There's no barrage fire on now, an' we ain't seen no grub for two whole days."

"Keep your heads down, lads."

The caution was hardly necessary. Each man was bent almost double. Over the parapet on the left a whiz-bang exploded, sending a shower of dirt upon the soldiers' steel helmets. Trench mortars were lobbing their deadly missiles into the British second-line trenches.

"Here you are," explained the guide as the head of the platoon emerged into a short "bay" or section of the winding trench. "Two men to each dug-out, sir; t'other fellows will show 'em the ropes better. C.O.'s dug-out is fifty yards further on, sir."

"Stick to me, Setley," whispered Alderhame.

"Will if I can," replied Ralph. "They're telling us off in pairs."

"You two in there," ordered a strange sergeant, indicating what appeared to be a glorified rabbit-hole burrowed out of the side of the trench. "New chums, mates," he continued, calling to the as yet invisible denizens of the subterranean dwelling.

"Come in," said a youthful voice. "Mind your head. I thought it was Dixon with the grub. Don't keep the curtain held back longer than usual. It isn't healthy, you know."

Down nine steps cut into the slippery clay, each succeeding step being a little more like liquid slime than the preceding one, Setley made his way, the top edge of his pack rubbing against the cross timbers of the roof of the obliquely sloping tunnel. His hand came in contact with a clammy ground-sheet, termed by courtesy a curtain. Pulling it aside he had his first vision of the interior of a dug-out—his temporary abode during his "turn" in the trenches. The excavation measured roughly twelve feet by nine, its height being barely sufficient to allow a tall man to stand upright. At the end furthest from the entrance was a stove fashioned out of an old tin bucket and provided with a decidedly inefficient chimney, since most of the fumes wafted into the dug-out. On the stove a "billy" was boiling. Stuck on the end of a flat piece of iron projecting from the wall was a guttering candle, the sole illumination, its yellow light being hardly powerful enough to penetrate the smoky atmosphere. Against a horizontal slab of wood reposed six rifles, while on slightly raised benches against the side walls were bundles of damp straw, rolled blankets and kit-bags.

"That's right," continued the voice that had bidden the strangers enter. "Sling your gear on that bench, and please don't trouble to wipe your boots. We didn't bother to polish the floor this morning."

Ridding himself of his rifle and pack, an example that Alderhame was quick to follow, Ralph turned his attention to his facetious new comrade.

By this time Setley had grown more accustomed to the dim light. Half lying, half sitting upon one of the benches was a mere lad of about nineteen or twenty, burly of figure, round-faced except for a pronounced hollow in his cheeks, and with dark brown eyes in which lurked a suspicion of constant mental strain. He had discarded his tunic, revealing a Cardigan jacket. Otherwise he was fully dressed, even to his muddy boots, from which the warm vapour rose like steam from the back of an overworked horse on a cold day. Pulled well down over his head was a grey woollen cap, while wrapped loosely round his neck was a khaki-coloured scarf.

"In the absence of a mutual friend to introduce us," remarked the recumbent occupant of the sleeping-place, "I suppose we must do the honours ourselves. My name's Penfold—No. 142857, which is jolly easy to remember if you know anything about recurring decimals. What's yours?"

Setley told him, adding gratuitously that he was a bank clerk.

"That so?" remarked Penfold. "I was in a shipping office. And your chum?"

"Alderhame is my name," replied the actor. "My profession? Well, I used to tread the boards."

"Strikes me you'll still tread the boards and feel jolly sick at doing it before long," rejoined Penfold with a laugh. "Duck-boards I mean. We were to have been relieved at eight this evening. Another regiment is supposed to take our place, but they didn't turn up. Why, I don't know; there wasn't much of a barrage this evening—and now the infernal racket is starting again."

Heavy shells exploding in front and behind the lines of trenches shook the dug-out until the timbering seemed in imminent danger of giving way.

For some moments there was silence in the underground refuge. The continuous crash without was appalling.

"Is this place shell-proof?" asked Alderhame.

"Nothing is," replied Penfold nonchalantly. "A direct hit with a big shell and it's 'Gone West' with the three of us. Hullo!"

The waterproof-sheet was drawn aside and a red-faced sergeant, the moisture running in rivulets from his steel helmet, thrust his head into the reeking dug-out.

"Look slippy, you chaps!" he exclaimed. "Every man is wanted. There's a massed attack developing."

CHAPTER III
THE NIGHT ATTACK

"Snatching up their rifles the three men hurried from the dug-out, nearly colliding with the rest of their chums who were returning

10

at the first alarm to get their equipment. "Follow me," exclaimed Penfold. "Keep well down."

At the fifth or sixth step along the tortuous communication trench Setley trod on something not so yielding as mud, but comparatively soft. He stooped and felt the object with his hand. His fingers came in contact with a human face.

"There's a man lying here!" he called out to Penfold, who was a few paces in front.

"I know," replied his new chum. "He's been there for the last three hours. Our fellows haven't had time to bring him in yet. Don't worry about that; you'll soon get used to it."

Setley hurried on, wondering whether he would ever get accustomed to the horrors of the trenches. The seemingly stony indifference with which Penfold had spoken jarred on his sensitive nerves. Somehow the realization did not fit in with the anticipation of what war really was. He could not help asking himself why nations should set about to deliberately exterminate each other merely for the lust of conquest—a wholesale slaughter by the most deadly scientific instrument that human ingenuity could devise.

His disjointed reveries were interrupted by Penfold being hurled violently backwards, his hunched shoulders striking Ralph violently in the chest. The two men staggered backwards, accompanied by showers of mud, stones, and displaced sand-bags, all silhouetted against the glare of an exploding shell. Three of the Wheatshires preceding Penfold were hurled bodily into the air, subsiding with sickening thuds upon the soft ground. One writhed furiously, groaning dismally the while; the others were mere lumps of clay fashioned in God's own image, but now hideously mangled.

"On!" exclaimed Penfold breathlessly. "Don't wait. The stretcher-bearers will be along for that fellow in half a shake."

Across a gap in the sand-bagged wall the men hurried. They could hear the hiss of the stream of bullets from a machine-gun. It seemed so close that Setley and Alderhame flung themselves flat.

"What are you hanging back for?" shouted a sergeant. "How the deuce can the rest of the men get by when you're blocking the road? Push along, both of you!"

Thus abjured the twain, fearing the scathing words of the N.C.O. more than the whistling bullets, slid over the mound of displaced sand-bags into the crater of the recently exploded shell, and scrambled up the other side.

Twenty paces more and Setley found himself in the front line trench. Almost mechanically he mounted the fire-step, rested the barrel of his rifle between two spaced sand-bags that formed a loophole, and waited.

"Here they come!" shouted an excited voice.

Standing out clearly against the glare of half a dozen star-shells came on dense masses of German infantry. The Huns advanced slowly, almost hesitatingly. There were no shouts of "Deutschland über alles!" that characterized the earlier attacks. The words were a hollow mockery—and the Huns knew it. They had now a wholesome respect for the British Tommy. It was mainly fear of their officers, who kept at the heels of their men and held revolvers ready to shoot down any who refused to charge, that made the attack develop.

In front came two men, masked and bearing metal cylinders resembling exaggerated packs upon their shoulders. In place of a rifle and bayonet they held a length of flexible hose. The Huns were about to use liquid fire in their attempt to oust the British from their trenches.

Supporting these perambulating torches were a dozen or more bombers, while close at their heels came men armed with rifles and bayonets. With the exception of the mud and numerous shell-craters there was little in the way of obstacles to impede their advance, for almost the whole of the wire entanglements fronting the British parapet had been blown away by shell-fire. Setley's impression at the unaccustomed sight was that the brunt of the attack was about to fall on his immediate front.

Suddenly the whole length of the British trench burst into a line of crackling flame as the Tommies commenced independent rapid fire. Some maxims, skilfully concealed in sand-bagged emplacements, added to the din with their quick pop-pop-pop.

The Huns, erroneously trusting that their heavy guns had battered the British trenches into shapeless mounds, and thinking that the Tommies had been either blown to fragments by the terrific artillery bombardment or had been compelled to seek refuge in their dug-outs, were met by the full blast of the rifle and machine-gun fire.

Ralph was soon surprised to find that he was slipping another clip of cartridges into the magazine of his rifle. He was now as cool as a cucumber. The months of infantry training had not been thrown away. With a visible enemy facing him he realized that the time had come when he could strike a blow for King and Country, instead of being subjected to shell-fire from a distant and unseen foe without being able to raise a hand in self-defence. The attack was doomed to failure from the start. One of the men bearing the liquid fire apparatus was on his face, his head and shoulders buried in mud, while his diabolical contrivance, which had evidently been perforated by a bullet, had taken fire and was blazing furiously. The bombers hurled their missiles prematurely, most of the bombs falling short; while the infantry, mown down in heaps, wavered, the survivors beginning to give way.

Above the rattle of musketry a whistle rang out loud and clear.

"Come on, boys!" shouted an officer, leaping on to the parapet, to topple backwards with a bullet through his brain.

Undeterred, the Wheatshires poured over the shattered breastwork of sand-bags. With an inspiring British cheer the infantry surged ver the top like a huge, irresistible breaker.

The opportune moment for delivering a counter-attack had arrived.

Well spent had been those months of active training. The Wheatshires, every man a passable athlete, literally swarmed over the parapet. With their bayonets gleaming in the ruddy glare and preceded by the regimental bombers the khaki-clad troops, dexterously threading their way through the gaps in the barbed wire, charged irresistibly against the already broken enemy.

A wave of thrilling enthusiasm swept over Private Setley. The chance of actually doing something, of getting clear of the imprisoning walls of slimy mire and coming to grips with the Hun had come. The studiously polite and law-abiding bank-clerk was transformed into a fighting Tommy. The lust of primeval combat was upon him. He saw red. Of what happened during the next two minutes Setley had but a faint and hazy notion. Bombs hurled by the retreating Huns fell around him. Once the blast from an exploding missile lifted his steel helmet from his head. He remembered putting it straight with his left hand and noticing that the fingers were covered with a dark, moist, warm fluid.

A man, keeping pace with him, suddenly dropped his rifle and fell on his face. Setley leapt over the slightly inclined bayonet and held on, the desire to stop and assist a fallen comrade being hardly existent. For the time being his sole desire was to overtake one of those field-grey forms showing dimly through the smoke.

The enemy first-line trenches at last—and the Huns were making a stand. A machine-gun, one of many, was pumping out nickel almost on Setley's immediate front. Hostile bombers were redoubling their efforts. In cold blood the lad would have thought twice, perhaps many times, before facing that deadly menace, but carried away in the mad rush he pressed forward, scarce noticing the weight of his rifle and bayonet.

13

A severed, coiled strand of barbed wire caught the puttee of his left foot. With a vicious jerk he freed himself from the encumbrance, leaving half a yard of mud-plastered cloth upon the sharp barb. Two yards in front of him was a burly German bomber with a bomb poised ready to hurl.

Regardless of the fact that the explosion of the missile would to an almost certainty annihilate him, the Hun threw the bomb. Setley caught it on the flat blade of his bayonet and threw it aside, where it burst ten yards to the right under a tall, bearded Prussian.

The next instant the thrower received six inches of cold steel right in the centre of his chest. Setley had made a mistake. It was a matter of considerable difficulty to withdraw the blade. He remembered too late the warning of the drill-instructors—when delivering a body thrust aim below the ribs.

Before he could disengage the steel another German commenced a furious blow with the butt-end of his rifle. In the midst of the swing of the weapon a shot rang out within a few inches of Setley's ear, and the Hun, with a curious look of surprise on his sullen features, staggered forward. The descending rifle-butt struck Setley's helmet a glancing blow and, missing his left shoulder, sank deeply into the mud.

"So much for Buckingham: off with his head," yelled Alderhame, as he ejected the still smoking cartridge-case from the breach of his rifle. "How's that, my festive?"

"Thanks," replied Setley briefly; then over the hostile parapet the two comrades surged, bending low as they crouched behind their ready bayonets.

The deep and narrow German trench was crowded with men—dead, wounded, and living. Some of the latter were putting up a stiff fight, like wild animals at bay. Others, with the dismal and monotonous whine of "Mercy, Kamerad!" were holding their hands high above their heads, the bombs taking toll of brave men and cowards alike.

Following at the heels of two of the Wheatshires' bombers, Setley, Alderhame, George Anderson, and two others, made their way along a traverse, the riflemen firing at the side of the bombers. At intervals the latter stopped to hurl their deadly missiles down the steep and steeply shelving entrances to the German dug-outs.

Rounding a sand-bagged traverse the party entered a bay in which was a machine-gun, with its crew of dead and dying lying around the silent weapon. A few paces further on a tall, bearded Hun barred the way.

"Hands up!" yelled Ginger.

14

The man threw down his rifle and complied. As the Tommies surged past Anderson took possession of the discarded weapon and tossed it over the parapet.

"Keep 'em up!" he continued, addressing his prisoner. "A little of that'll do you no 'arm. You bide 'ere till you're told to shift."

A shot rang out, and one of the British bombers dropped. His companion hurled a bomb, while Setley and Alderhame pushed forward towards a temporary barrier of sand-bags hastily piled on the floor of the trench. Beyond were three Huns, one of whom had just fired the fatal shot; but the avenging bomb had already done its work.

Standing on the parados was a captain of the Wheatshires.

"Back, men!" he ordered. "Don't get out of touch with the rest of the company. Secure your prisoners and retire."

"Retire, be hanged!" muttered George. "Wot's to prevent us going on to Berlin? Eh, you treacherous swine, wot's the game?"

He clapped his hand to his ear. One portion of the lobe was missing. The man he had taken prisoner had drawn a small revolver from his pocket and had fired at five paces at his captor while the latter's back was turned.

With a yell Ginger rushed at the recreant Hun. Once more the man's hands were raised above his head, and again the dolorous "Mercy, Kamerad; me haf wife and six children!"

"Liar!" shouted the now furious Tommy, giving the treacherous Boche a generous amount of cold steel. "You've a widow an' six orphans!"

Reluctantly, the Wheatshires quitted the hostile trenches and made their way back across No Man's Land. In many cases their officers had to push them towards their own lines. Having made good their footing in the German defences, the Tommies did not relish the idea of abandoning the ground. It did not occur to them that the captured trench would form a dangerous salient, liable to be enfiladed and levelled flat with hostile shells before it could be properly consolidated.

"How about grub?" enquired Penfold, as the men regained the safety of their own lines. "There's no barrage now? Why can't they bring our tommy up to us?"

"Could do with a good meal myself," said Sefton. "Fortunately, we were served out with bully-beef before we arrived. You can have some of mine."

"Thanks, awfully," replied his new chum. "I'll accept; but, remember, it's bad policy. Generosity is all very well, but here it's each man for himself in the grub line. You can't blame a half-starving fellow sneaking any food that he finds lying about, you know."

"How is it that you're short of rations?" asked Alderhame.

"Goodness only knows. The Huns were going it pretty hot all day and during the earlier part of this evening. Perhaps our ration party copped it. Everything has to be brought up by hand in this section of the line," replied Penfold. "Well, let's foot it, before the guns start again. The Boches will be pretty wild after this little affair."

Mingled with a jostling throng of exultant Tommies and dejected prisoners, the three made their way along the communication trench to their dug-out.

"What luck!" ejaculated Penfold, stopping short at a heap of disordered sand-bags and splintered timber that marked the site of their temporary abode. "Our dug-out has been properly strafed. We would have all gone West by this time if we'd been inside. But I say, you fellows; what price grub, now?"

CHAPTER IV
GRUB

"Penfold spoke of his escape without emotion. He had been long enough check by jowl with death to express no surprise. He had merely remarked that it was a lucky chance that the occupants of the shelled dug-out had not been inside when the heavy howitzer missile had demolished it. What did seriously annoy him was the loss of the promised food.

Ralph Setley, although by this time ravenously hungry, was fervently thankful for his escape. Already the reaction of the raid into the German trenches was beginning to tell. Shorn of excitement of the wild rush over the top, the horrors of that nocturnal excursion rose up in his mind. The knowledge that he had bayoneted a fellow-creature, although he were an enemy and a brutal Hun, worried him.

"Suppose the fellow would have done me in if I hadn't got him first," he soliloquized. Then, aloud:

"What are you jabbering about, Alderhame?"

The former actor was stamping up and down the duck-boards, now encrusted with a thin coating of ice:—

"Freeze, freeze, thou bitter sky,

16

Thou dost not bite so nigh
As benefits forgot."

"That's As You Like It! chum. It aptly describes our condition. Horribly cold, and benefits in the shape of bully-beef gone, though not forgotten. Where's our next lodging?"

The stream of prisoners and wounded Tommies had now dwindled. Penfold, addressing a sergeant, stated his case.

"D'ye think I'm a Cook's tourist guide?" snapped the N.C.O. "Turn in where you can. There are a good many half empty dug-outs now, I'm thinking."

A shell shrieked overhead. The Huns were putting up a barrage, the shrapnel falling amongst their own men, who, prisoners in the hands of the British, were being escorted to the "Advance cages."

"In here," said Penfold, making a dive for the nearest entrance. Alderhame followed close at his heels, then Setley and George Anderson, the latter still grousing at the loss of a quarter of an inch of his ear.

"Anyone at home?" enquired Penfold.

He pushed aside the covering to the sloping tunnel and entered the dug-out, which in point of size and contents was much the same as his demolished mud-hole—the damp steaming straw, the pungent fumes of the charcoal brazier, the moisture dripping through the timber-shored roof, and the guttering candle—a typical Tommy's barrack-room on the Somme Front.

Seated on an upturned ammunition-case and with his feet resting on another tin box, in order to keep them out of the slime, was a young, pale-faced, dark-haired soldier He was busily engaged in writing with an indelible pencil certain words of deeper violet hue, betraying the fact that the paper shared the general failing of the subterranean abode—it was moist: uncommonly so.

So engrossed was the writer that for some moments he "carried on" with his task. Then looking up, and seeing strange faces, he exclaimed, in a lisping drawl:

"I say, you've made a mistake. This isn't your caboodle."

"No mistake, chummy," replied Penfold firmly. "We've been shelled out. We crave your hospitality. How many men in this dug-out?"

"There were eight this morning," replied the youth:

"Where are the others?"

"Ask me another."

"I will," rejoined Penfold, depositing his rifle on a bench. "Have they left any grub?"

17

"Wish they had," was the grim answer. Then, with more eagerness than he had hitherto shown, he asked: "Have you any food? I haven't had a bite since this morning. Finished the whole of my ration, including jam, thinking that the fresh stuff would be in— but it isn't!"

"You're welcome to a share of ours, laddie," remarked Alderhame, "which happens to be nixes."

Ralph sat down on a bundle of straw, having first appropriated the late occupant's pack as a pillow. He was feeling horribly tired. His feet and hands were numbed with the cold. His saturated clothes were throwing off wisps of muggy vapour. Even a huge rat pattering on the muddy floor and scampering through the straw hardly troubled him, and a few hours previously he would have gone twenty yards to avoid one.

In his drowsiness he found himself contemplating the latest of his many new comrades.

"I'll bet that chap's a Jew," he thought.

Setley was right in his surmise. Sidney Bartlett was the grandson of a Polish refugee who had become a naturalized Englishman and, dropping the name of Bariniski, had successfully engaged in business in Birmingham. Like many of the Hebrew race, young Bartlett was a patriot and a staunch supporter of the land of his adoption. When the call to arms came he rallied to the Colours, only to be sent back until he was sufficiently old to serve in His Majesty's Forces. Only three years previously Sidney was at a large day school, and there occurred an incident that was to influence his conduct at the Somme Front.

For some weeks the lad was persistently absent from school. The head master constantly received notes to the effect that Sidney was kept at home through domestic troubles, in which a grandmother figured largely. The caligraphy arousing his suspicions, the head wrote to the lad's father, and then the "cat was out of the bag."

One afternoon Bartlett Senior, accompanied by his errant son, came to the head master's study.

"Now, Sidney," said his sire, solemnly, "I vant you to tell de trut'—de whole trut', mind. Later on, in bizness, Sidney, you may tell a lie; but now you must tell de trut'."

Utterly worn out, Setley fell asleep—a slumber broken with dreams of the exciting episodes of the last few hours. Rats wandered at will over his couch of straw; vermin of other kind swarmed everywhere. His companions, too hungry to sleep, sat up and smoked, recounting anecdotes on almost every topic except the war.

18

Without the guns thundered incessantly, but the duel was chiefly betwixt the artillery, and the trenches were left almost untouched.

"I'm off to see if I can't find some grub," declared Penfold. "Who's game?"

Ginger Anderson volunteered to accompany him with the greatest alacrity. It was better than sitting still in a damp dug-out with hunger gnawing at one's vitals. Alderhame and Bartlett also expressed their willingness to take part in the foraging expedition.

"I reckon as if we do 'ave any luck," remarked Ginger, "the rations will arrive directly we do, and all our work'll be for nothing."

"So much the better," rejoined Penfold.

"How about Setley?"

"Let him sleep on," suggested the ex-actor:

"Why rather, sleep, liest thou in smoky cribs
Upon uneasy pallets stretching thee,
And hush'd with buzzing night-flies to thy slumber."

"'Buzzing night-flies' sounds poetical," remarked Penfold. "Poetic licence shows tactful discretion in this case. Come along, you fellows."

The four adventurers sallied forth to beg, borrow, or steal something in the edible line. It was freezing so hard that the trench-boards were immovably cemented in solid mud of the hardness of stone.

"Thank goodness we weren't warned for the wiring party," whispered Penfold. "Black as pitch, and as cold as charity. Hist! What do you make of that?"

He pointed to a faint ray of light emanating from an oblique shaft of a dug-out—that of the major of his company. The opening was for ventilating purposes, and was fitted with a piece of corrugated iron to prevent the water making its way into the underground room. From the shaft came the unmistakable odour of roast meat.

One by one the men reconnoitred, and withdrew to a safe distance to deliberate.

"Regular old food-hog," declared Alderhame. "Not only is he about to wolf a pound of meat, but there's a pudding and a packet of sausages. Presumably, his missis has sent him out a hamper."

"Too much for one man, albeit a field officer," decided Penfold. "Lads, we must have some of that grub!"

"'Ow?" enquired Anderson. "Yer can't just pop in an' say, friendly like: 'Wot cheer, major, old sport; 'ow abart it? Can yer?"

"Can't we lure him out?" suggested Alderhame.

"We might; but what's the use?" rejoined Penfold. "These

officers' dug-outs have doors, and ten to one he'll lock it if he goes far from his grub."

"You get him out," said Sidney Bartlett. "I'll do the rest. All we want is a light pole. There are some in the next traverse. Lash a bayonet to one end and spear what we can through that hole."

"Sounds feasible," agreed Penfold. "Nip off and get the gear ready."

In a short space of time Bartlett had rigged up his improvised fishing-tackle.

"Now," he said, "I'm ready. You carry on, Penfold."

Drawing his woollen cap well over his eyes and turning up the collar of his greatcoat as high as possible, Penfold knocked at the door of the Major's dug-out.

"Well?" enquired a deep muffled voice testily.

"Colonel's compliments, sir," announced the mendacious private, in an assumed tone. "He wants you to report to him at once upon the number of men left in this section of the trench."

Grumbling, the Major issued from his subterranean retreat, carefully locked the door, and set out to find the company sergeant-major, in order to obtain the supposedly urgent information.

Before he returned the four raiders were scurrying back to their dug-out, each with his mouth full of cold sausage, while Alderhame retained a painful impression of an otherwise appetizing repast in the shape of a cut on his cheek, caused by the end of the pole as the elated Sidney swiftly withdrew it with the prized booty impaled upon the bayonet.

"Where's my first-aid dressing?" enquired the ex-actor, with mock concern.

"'And patches will I get unto these scars
And swear I got them in the Gallia wars.'"

"Hardly good enough for Blighty," said Penfold, with a laugh. "My word, won't the Major be in a tear when he misses his sausages!"

"Let him," said Bartlett. "He can only blame the rats."

"Halt! Who goes there?" exclaimed the hoarse voice of a sentry in the next traverse.

"Engineers' ration party," was the reply. "Is this the Royal Engineers?"

"Rather!" replied the ready Penfold. "Dump 'em down; we'll fetch them."

Out of the neighbouring dug-outs poured other Tommies. Without having any suspicion of the ruse played upon them, the ration party handed over the stores intended for a company of the

Royal Engineers, who were engaged in tunnelling on the left of the Wheatshires' trenches. Almost in the nick of time a famine was averted at the expense of the sappers and miners. But, as Penfold remarked, it was each man for himself when it came to a case of semi-starvation.

CHAPTER V
THE EXPEDITION TO NO MAN'S LAND

""Turn out, you chaps! You're warned for duty in the first-line trench."

With the sergeant's words ringing in his ears Ralph Setley arose from his uncomfortable bed. A candle was still guttering. It was not yet dawn. The Huns' protracted shelling had ceased until the time for their customary morning "hate."

The rest of the occupants of his dug-out were engaged upon their morning "toilet"—the rite consisting of cleaning and oiling their rifles. Washing was out of the question, and as they had turned in fully dressed, including great-coats and boots, there was nothing further to be done beyond cooking breakfast.

Thanks to the blunder of the rationing party the men regaled themselves with slices of bacon, bread not more than three days old, and tea of exceptionally strong brew. The bacon was gritty, which was not to be wondered at, seeing that the men had been under shell-fire almost the whole way to the trenches.

Alderhame was in high spirits notwithstanding he had had but a few hours' sleep. There was a touch of the far-off "green-room" days, as he laid his hand on Setley's shoulder.

"Come on, laddie," he said. "Let's survey the radiant morn:—
"This battle fares like to the morning's war,
    When dying clouds contend with glowing light;
What time the shepherd, blowing of his nails,
    Can neither call it perfect day nor night."

Viewed in the pale grey dawn, the dreary stretch of No Man's Land was robbed of most of its ghastly details. Here and there, often in heaps, huddled corpses dressed in mud-stained field-grey testified to the accuracy of the British rifle and machine-gun fire. Further away lay the trenches that the Wheatshires had visited so effectively. Already Hun wiring parties had been out, and the shattered stakes and snake-like coils of severed barbed wire had been replaced by new. Almost in the front row of wire a black, white, and red striped flag—the emblem of Germany—fluttered in the faint breeze.

Setley could now understand why the order for recall had been given when the regiment was in possession of this section of the Hun trenches, for dominating the advance works was a strong redoubt, known to the Wheatshires by the somewhat ominous name of Pumpnickel. For the last three weeks the Engineers—the same company whose rations had been appropriated by the Wheatshires—had been engaged in driving a mine-gallery in the direction of this earthwork-fortress. Great things were promised when the time came to spring the mine and send Pumpnickel Redoubt flying in the air.

"I mean to get that flag," declared Bartlett. "I'll go out to-night and bring it in."

"Wouldn't if I were you," said Penfold. "It's a sort of booby-trap, I wouldn't mind betting. Something that, when moved, explodes a grenade."

"I'll risk that," declared the lad grimly. "The Boches mustn't flaunt their colours in our faces. I was——"

Something "pinged" on the rounded surface of his steel helmet. A watchful sniper had seized his chance. Only by an inch had Sidney escaped death, for had the bullet struck the steel squarely instead of glancing off the convex surface the head-gear would not have withstood the impact.

"Are you young fools looking for trouble?" growled Sergeant Ferris, the N.C.O. who had routed them from the dug-out. "Keep under cover, and use a trench periscope if you want to enjoy the scenery."

"Thanks for the tip, sergeant," said George Anderson. "Sorry I can't offer yer a seegar, sergeant; I left me case on the grand pianner at 'ome; but 'ave a fag—a genuine Day's March Nearer 'Ome' brand."

The N.C.O. took the proffered cigarette and lit it slowly and deliberately.

"Are we on Wiring Party to-night, sergeant?" asked Ginger.

"Not as I know of," was the reply. "Why?"

"'Cause my pal 'ere is goin' to get 'old of that striped bed-cover"—jerking his thumb in the direction of the German flag—"an' I'm a-goin' with 'im; ain't I, Sid, ole sport?"

"Then you'll have to be sharp about it," remarked Sergeant Ferris. "The mine is to be sprung at 3.30 a.m. We're over the top again; this time there'll be no going back, if all goes well. We ought to advance four hundred yards and consolidate the position. So now

22

you know. Go for the flag at your own risk, chums; but don't forget. Be back before three, or you'll stand a sure and certain chance of going to Kingdom Come with a couple o' hundred perishing Boches for company."

During the rest of the day nothing happened beyond the customary routine of trench life, combined with the monotonous occurrence of casualties.

"Are you still of the same mind, Bartlett?" enquired Alderhame, as darkness set in.

"Rather," was the firm reply.

"Then I'm going with you."

"And I," added Setley.

"No, you don't," objected Anderson. "Two's quite enough for this blessed job. Look 'ere: if I don't come back, there's a letter in my pack wot I wants sent 'ome. Anythink else you can 'ave, fags an' all. I'm going to 'ave a doss. Turn me out at twelve."

"Rum chap," commented Alderhame, indicating the soundly sleeping Ginger. "A regular rough diamond, always ready to do a pal a good turn."

"By the by," said Setley. "You did me a good turn when my bayonet got hung up, although you nearly split the drum of my ear when you fired and brought down the fellow who was about to club me."

"Every little helps," said Alderhame. "Lucky for you the Hun wasn't on my left side."

"Why?" enquired Ralph curiously.

"Simply because I'm stone-blind in my left eye," replied the ex-actor composedly. "I was passed for Class A just the same. When I told the doctor he merely remarked: 'Oh, left eye, eh? Well, a man almost invariably shoots with his right eye!' 'I'd sooner shoot with a rifle, sir!' I said. 'And so you shall, my man!' he rejoined, laughing at my repartee; so he marked me down for general service, and here I am. I'm not at all sorry. If I come through this business it will be something to be proud of, you know."

All was quiet between the opposing lines. The Huns, realizing the superior weight and volume of fire of the British guns, wisely refrained from inviting them; while the latter, massed until they were practically wheel to wheel, were silent, concentrating their energies for a terrific tornado of shell as a prelude to the rush of the infantry "over the top."

At midnight the two volunteers were roused from their slumbers.

"Still of the same mind?" enquired Penfold.

"Not 'arf," replied Ginger, while Bartlett nodded his head and shrugged his shoulders in the characteristic way that he had inherited from his Polish ancestors.

"We'll speed the parting guests," declared Alderhame, with a forced attempt at joviality. "Me lud, your carriage waits."

"Chuck it!" retorted Anderson. "'Ere, gimme me baynit. Look arter me rifle till I comes back. Now, Sidney, old sport."

Setley, Penfold, and the ex-actor accompanied them to the front trench. Like men about to dive into icy-cold water the two raiders paused, with one foot on the fire-step; then without a word both wriggled silently and cautiously over the parapet. Ten seconds later the intense darkness had swallowed them up.

Braving the piercing cold the three men awaited their comrades' return, peering at intervals over the top of the parapet and straining their ears to catch the faintest sound of their movements. Twenty minutes passed, but neither by sight nor sound did the twain betray their presence in the forbidding No Man's Land.

Suddenly the darkness was pierced by a short shriek of mingled pain and rage, the thud of blows falling on some soft object, and the unmistakable squelching of many feet in the tenacious slime.

"Good heavens!" ejaculated Penfold. "They've been done in. Who's going out, lads?"

"Not much use at present," objected Alderhame. "The Huns are on the alert. When things have quieted down a bit, I'll go."

"That's the spirit, lad," said Sergeant Ferris, who had joined the party of watchers. "Discretion is what's wanted now. We've chucked away two men over this business already, and all for the sake of a dirty German flag."

Another twenty minutes passed. The Huns could be heard talking excitedly in their trenches, but the distance was too great to distinguish their words. Setley was of the opinion that Sidney was a prisoner. He fancied that he heard the lad's voice, but he could not be certain.

"If they'd got Ginger," declared Penfold, "there would be no doubt of hearing his voice. Well, lads, are you fit?"

The three men began to remove great-coats and everything likely to impede their movements. Suddenly Setley snatched up his rifle.

"What's up, now?" asked the sergeant.

"Something moving," declared the lad.

The sentries, too, held their arms in readiness to open fire.

"Steady on, chums," whispered Ginger. "Don't let rip. It's only me."

He wriggled over the parapet and dropped inertly upon the fire-step. For some moments he lay like one dead, his comrades forbearing to question him.

Presently he raised his head, and extending his hand showed a closely rolled bundle that was indistinguishable in the darkness.

"I've got it, mates," he announced. "It's the flag we went out for. Got me baynit into one bloke's throat, an' didn't 'e scream."

"Where's Sidney?" asked Penfold.

"Ain't 'e back? I lost touch with 'im. 'Ere, I'm off out again!"

"No, you don't," declared Sergeant Ferris firmly. "You'll be put under arrest if you attempt it. You're done up. Now, you fellows, if you're going you'd best look sharp about it. Take a rope, in case you find young Bartlett. Slip it round his heels, and drag him in if he cannot crawl."

In spite of his resolution, Setley's heart was literally in his mouth when he found himself in contact with the slime of No Man's Land. At ten paces he had lost all idea of the whereabouts of his companions. Guided by the relative position of the Pole star, now shining feebly through the drifting smoke, he crawled slowly but steadily onwards towards the spot where the coveted flag had been planted.

At frequent intervals star-shells burst overhead, throwing a blinding, ghostly glare upon the crater-pitted ground. Their appearance was the signal for Setley to throw himself flat upon the ground. The slightest movement would have resulted in a machine-gun being trained upon him. With his face pillowed on his arm—it was the only way of preventing a smothering acquaintance with the evil-smelling Somme mud—he was unable to take advantage of the light to look for his companions. Whether they were ahead, behind, or had relinquished their efforts, he was totally in ignorance.

Presently his hand came in contact with some hard cold substance. It was the face of a frozen corpse—that of a Hun, judging by the cloth-swathed helmet. The man was obviously a sniper, for he had on him a stock of candles, food and drink, and a pair of binoculars. Evidently he was making, under cover of darkness, for a favourite lair when a chance bullet struck him on the forehead.

A searchlight, unexpectedly unmasked, swept the ground. Fortunately, Setley had just crept into a shell-crater, and the raised lip effectually intercepted the dazzling rays. From the corner of his eye he made out the sinister lines of wire fronting the German trenches, the criss-cross of barbed entanglements standing out like silver filigree work in the cold rays of the electric light. He was within a few feet of his objective.

Voices were talking just over the sand-bagged parapet. He listened. There were Germans speaking in broken English, asking questions in menacing tones. Someone was answering—and that someone was Private Sidney Bartlett.

CHAPTER VI
A PRISONER OF WAR

"An almost similar pilgrimage across No Man's Land had been made by Private Bartlett, but with a different ending. Before he was aware of the fact he had blundered into a party of Germans engaged in wiring the defences, and as he made a vicious jab with his bayonet at the nearest of the Huns he was felled with a blow of a mallet. Without a cry he dropped senseless.

In an unconscious condition he was brought in by his captors, and placed unceremoniously on the fire-step of the hostile trench. At the first sign of the prisoner's senses returning his guards sent word to their officers that the Englishman was recovering and could be interrogated.

"Now you vos tell me der truth," said the German menacingly. "Der whole truth, mind, or we vos haf you shot. I know plenty about your trenches, so if you tell der lie den I vos you find out. Now, vot regiment you vos?"

"The Wheatshires," replied the captive promptly. He knew that the Huns were fully aware of the composition of the troops engaged opposite to them.

"Goot!" said the Major. "Dot vos so. Now, der is talk of und mine. Dot is so?"

"Yes," replied Sidney. "We have sunk a mine gallery."

"In vot direction?" was the next question.

Sidney paused to think. He recalled his father's words. "In business, Sidney, you can tell a lie." This was a business—one of the grimmest businesses that fall to the lot of men and nations— scientific murder, licensed under the name of war.

"Why you no answer?" prompted the Hun.

"Suppose I refuse?" asked the captive. "Men taken prisoner are not compelled to reply to questions on military matters."

The German laughed gruffly.

"Rules of war for fools are," he chuckled. "We Germans make war, we no play. You answer vill make now, so."

"All right; if I am compelled to do so," rejoined Sidney. "The mine runs away to your left—two hundred yards, I should think." In point of fact, and Private Bartlett was perfectly aware of it, the explosion chamber was almost immediately beyond that part of the hostile trench in which he was held prisoner. Although the main force of the explosion would be directed against the Pumpnickel Redoubt there was the almost certainty of a swift and terrible death to every living creature in the German first-line trenches as well.

The Hun officer snapped out some words of command to his men. The soldiers began to pile up sand-bags across the trench to neutralize, as they thought, the outlying effects of the impending explosion, while the locality that Bartlett had purposely and wrongly indicated was cleared of troops.

"Ach!" continued the Major. "Now you vos tell me dis: at vot hour the mine goes it off?"

"At six-thirty," replied Sidney promptly. He was entering eagerly into the "business" by this time. It would result, he had no doubt, in the extermination of several hundred Germans and his comparatively insignificant self as well.

"Now, we see," remarked the Prussian officer. "If der truth you haf said, den all vill well be. We keep you here—in der drench."

Evidently the German had certain misgivings, for, ordering a post to be driven deeply into the slime and his prisoner to be firmly bound to it, he scurried off to a remote portion of the reserve trenches.

This much Ralph Setley heard. From other sounds he came to the conclusion that most, if not all, of the German troops were following their superior's example.

"Time for me to be getting back," he soliloquized. "There may yet be an opportunity for our chaps to raid the trench and rescue Bartlett before the mine is sprung. Wonder how time goes? It seems as if I've been out for a couple of hours."

He returned in quicker time than he had taken to crawl out to the barbed wire entanglements. For one thing the Huns were no longer in the trench, ready to train a machine-gun on any moving object that they were able to discern in the glare of the star-shells. For another thing, the artillery duel had increased in violence, the rain of projectiles from the British guns being unmistakably superior in velocity to that of the Huns. Perhaps it was a prelude to the impending advance? If so, the hour fixed for the firing of the mine was at hand.

"That you, Setley?" came a hoarse whisper almost into his ear.

"Yes," replied Ralph, recognizing Alderhame's voice.

"Thought you had been done in. We've been back some time. I crawled out to see if I could find you. Come along."

A rifle-bullet whizzed past Setley's head.

Promptly he ducked and crouched in a convenient shell-hole. Somewhere in No Man's Land a Hun sniper was on the qui vive.

A dozen shots rang out from the British trenches in reply. The flash of the sniper's rifle had betrayed his position. A squeal, like that of a stuck pig, showed pretty plainly that the Hun ought to have stopped a bullet.

The noise was but a ruse on the sniper's part, for as Alderhame and Setley scrambled over the parapet another shot rang out from the same spot, the bullet grazing the heel of Ralph's boot and cutting a slight furrow on his wrist.

It was hard lines on the sniper; for just as he fired his second shot a German shell, falling short—as defective projectiles are apt to do—landed fairly on top of his lair. In the flash that followed the luckless sniper's body was hurled high in the air, and fell with a sickening thud almost on top of the British parapet.

"What have you been up to?" enquired Sergeant Ferris.

Briefly, Setley told the non-com. of what he had heard.

"Then come along and report to the Colonel," continued the sergeant. "By smoke, if we get permission to attempt a rescue every man-jack in the battalion will want to be over the top."

"A very creditable performance," declared the officer commanding the Wheatshires, when Ralph had made his report. "Private Bartlett is a brick. No; I do not think it advisable to go out again. The hostile wire is now intact, I understand. As things go we must leave Bartlett to take his chances. It would be madness to throw even a platoon against standing entanglements. One must not allow sentiment to jeopardize men's lives."

Somewhat crestfallen, Sergeant Ferris and Private Setley left the C.O.'s dug-out. It was now half-past two—the time fixed for the men to assemble for the task of occupying and consolidating the mine-crater.

Like ghostly forms the steel-helmeted Tommies clustered in the fire-trench. The officers, nervously consulting their watches at every half-minute, felt the tedious wait as acutely as the men. Once the whistle blew the excitement of the wild rush would come as a welcome relief to the dreary and nerve-racking period of waiting, when men have opportunities to conjure up mental pictures of what might happen during the dash across No Man's Land.

"Ain't it about time that blinkin' mine went up?" whispered George Anderson. "Ain't it perishin' cold? If I 'ave to wait much longer I won't 'ave no feet to carry me over the top."

"Five minutes longer," announced Penfold. "Hullo! What's up with the company on our right flank?"

The men referred to could be seen filing off along the narrow trench. In half a minute the three adjacent bays were deserted, except for the sentries and the men told off for duty in the firing line.

A subaltern floundered along the duck-boards and whispered to the platoon commander.

The charge was to be deferred pending further orders from headquarters. Either something had gone wrong with the final preparations of the mine, or else information had been received that necessitated the advance being postponed.

"Turn in, you fellows," said Sergeant Ferris. "No more going out to-night! Sorry for young Bartlett, but you know what the Colonel said."

"'Ow about our relief, sergeant?" enquired George Anderson. "Thought the Wheatshires were to be sent back last night?"

"Don't know as you've much cause to grumble," replied the N.C.O., "seeing that you haven't been twenty-four hours in the firing trench. Some of the boys have had six days of it."

"Seems like twenty-four months, sergeant," continued Ginger.

"P'r'aps; but you're a glutton for going out over No Man's Land," said Ferris. "You've no call to complain that it hasn't been exciting enough."

"A chap must do something to keep himself warm," groused the private, as he followed Setley and Alderhame to their now depleted dug-out.

CHAPTER VII
THE FIRST ADVANCE

""My eye, you chaps! Come out and have a look," exclaimed Penfold, who, having gone to draw rations for the rest of the occupants of the dug-out, had just returned with a generous quantity of tea, bacon, and comparatively fresh loaves.

"Look at what?" asked Alderhame, still stretched on his bed of damp straw. "The dawn——?"

29

"At what those strafed Huns have done," declared Penfold.

"If it's young Sidney they've been doing in there'll be trouble," declared Alderhame.

The quartette left their subterranean retreat and made their way to the fire-trench. By means of a trench periscope they surveyed the hostile lines. Above the sand-bags was a rough notice-board on which was chalked:

"OTHER COMRADS WELKOME."

A fusillade of rifle bullets quickly demolished the offending board, but almost immediately it was replaced by another:

"WHEN ARE YOU ENGLANDER COMING? WE
ARE TIRED OF WATEING FOR THE ADVANCE
PROMISED."

This, too, was speedily shot to pieces, and having let off a considerable quantity of "hot air" the Tommies returned to their breakfasts.

At ten o'clock the men crowded into the fire-trench. Although no information had been given out concerning the revised arrangements for the attack the men instinctively realized that the crucial moment was at hand.

Suddenly the desultory cannonade gave place to a violent artillery bombardment, to which the German guns could do little or nothing in reply. Admirably registered, their range being regulated either by observation officers at isolated posts or else from the aeroplanes that hovered overhead, the shells battered the Hun wire entanglements and first-line trenches almost out of recognition. The air was filled with dust and smoke—red, yellow, and green in colour—while through the clouds of vapour could be discerned the dismembered bodies of German soldiers hurled twenty feet or more into the air by the terrific force of the exploding missiles.

For a solid twenty minutes the hail of high explosive projectiles continued, while simultaneously shrapnel put up a barrage in the rear of the hostile trenches with a two-fold purpose: to prevent the Huns running away and also to make it almost impossible for reinforcements to be brought up to the firing line.

"They're lifting!" exclaimed Penfold as the shells began to drop further away.

"Five minutes more, lads!" said the platoon commander in clear, decisive tones. "Now, show them what the Wheatshires can do in broad daylight."

"D'ye want a leg-up, Tubby?" sang out George Anderson, addressing his remarks to a corpulent private whose previous efforts to surmount the parapet were ludicrous in spite of the mental and physical strain of "going over the top."

A general laugh greeted George's words, the butt of his remarks joining in the hilarity. With few exceptions the men were high-spirited. Their confidence in the artillery and the knowledge that they were "top-dog" when it came to hand-to-hand fighting made them eager and alert to rush forward at the first blast of the whistle.

Thirty seconds more.

With an ear-splitting roar and a veritable volcano of flame the mine under the Pumpnickel Redoubt was exploded. The earth trembled violently with the crash of the detonation. In places sand-bags slipped bodily into the British trench. A gust of violently displaced air, bearing grit and dust, mingled with weightier fragments, swept over the heads of the waiting Tommies. Where the strongly fortified earthworks had stood was a crater quite two hundred yards across, but how deep the British were yet to learn.

Before the last of the far-flung debris had fallen to earth the whistles sounded. With a rousing cheer the line of khaki-clad men swarmed over the parapet into the muddy and smoke-laden, crater-pitted No Man's Land.

Almost without opposition the Wheatshires gained their objective. More, carried away by their enthusiasm, pressed onwards, until their officers, realizing that the men were in danger of being hit by their own shells, recalled them with difficulty.

Lining the outer edge of the enormous mine-crater, the Wheatshires set to work to consolidate their easily won position. Setley, while engaged in the work, viewed with astonishment the stupendous result of the explosion of the mine. For full seventy feet the scorched and still smoking earth sloped steeply to the bottom of the immense pit. Everything of a defensive nature—concrete gun-pits, reinforced trenches, and deep dug-outs—was obliterated by the comparatively smooth "batter" of displaced chalk and earth.

"When are the guns going to lift, do you think, sergeant?" asked Penfold, who, having laid aside his rifle, was piling up sand-bags with the energy of a steam-engine.

"'Bout time," replied Sergeant Ferris. "We're supposed to make good for a mile. Hullo! What's happening on our left flank?"

Setley glanced in the direction indicated by the non-com. Here the Coalshires, many obliquely to the general line of advance, were falling in heaps. Men were tugging and hacking frantically at formidable barriers of uncut barbed wire. Evidently this section of the hostile line had escaped the otherwise general pulverization of the Hun entanglements, while the enemy, quick to grasp the advantage, had brought up dozens of machine-guns from deep dug-outs, raising the intact weapons to the surface by means of lifts.

"Good God!" ejaculated Alderhame hoarsely. "Our fellows are giving way."

With almost every officer either killed or wounded, confronted by an almost insurmountable barrier of barbed wire, and subjected to a terrific hail of machine-gun fire the Coalshires were almost decimated. Bodies, riddled with bullets, were hanging from the wire, their clothing held by the tenacious barbs. Contradictory orders added to the confusion, while to make matters worse the Huns began firing gas-shells into the wavering troops.

The quick eye of the Wheatshires' Colonel took in the situation. Another regiment, hitherto held in reserve, was advancing to assist in the holding of the mine-crater in anticipation of the usual counter-attack. For the time being the reinforcements must make good the advantage won by the battalion already in possession of the position.

At the word of command the Wheatshires swung out of the captured crater and charged the flank of that part of the German trenches left intact.

Almost before he realized it Setley found himself in a traverse, the furthermost end of which was packed with Huns, whose attention was mainly directed upon the disordered Coalshires on their immediate front.

With bayonet and bomb the attackers cleared the front three bays of the trench, the surviving Germans either bolting from their dug-outs or throwing up their hands with the now familiar cry of "Mercy, Kamerad."

Briefly the situation was as follows. On a front of nearly four miles the British had advanced a distance averaging eight hundred yards with the exception of half a mile of trenches before which the Coalshires had been held up. This section, strongly defended, was a tough nut to be cracked, but now surrounded on three sides, the Huns had either the option to resist to the last man or surrender. For the present they chose the former alternative, conscious that by holding out they were deferring the general advance of the British troops.

"Clear those dug-outs!" shouted a captain to No. 3 Platoon. Experience had taught him the inadvisability of leaving a nest of armed Huns behind the advancing Tommies.

"Out you come!" shouted Alderhame, flattening himself against the concrete sides of the first dug-out and pointing his rifle down the flight of steps leading to the deep subterranean retreat.

With his bayonet at the "ready" Setley took up his stand at the opposite side and awaited the result of his comrade's challenge, while George Anderson covered the mouth of the dug-out with a Mills bomb. "Ja! We come!" shouted a guttural voice from the deep recesses.

"And be mighty sharp about it," rejoined Alderhame.

But instead of the head of a procession of grey-coated Huns with upheld hands a bomb came hurtling from the dug-out. With the fuse sizzling briskly the missile dropped midway between Setley and the ex-actor.

In a trice Alderhame threw himself flat upon the ground. Setley, hardly realizing the danger, stood stockstill, his bayonet still directed towards the mouth of the dug-out. In another second——

With a muffled bang the bomb exploded. Ralph had a momentary vision of a khaki-clad Tommy being lifted five or six feet from the ground and subsiding almost at his feet. Simultaneously George Anderson hurled his missile straight into the cavernous recesses of the dug-out with disastrous results to the former occupants. "'Urt?" enquired Ginger laconically, as he assisted the fallen Tommy to his feet. It was Penfold, dazed and shaken, but otherwise unhurt.

Seeing the bomb lying on the ground Penfold, with admirable presence of mind, snatched up a sand-bag, threw it upon the missile and had held it in position until the explosion took place. This sand-bag resisted the disastrous effect of the bomb, although the detonation was sufficient to blow the intrepid Penfold some feet into the air.

"Good for the D.C.M.," yelled Alderhame. "Come on, lads. Let's see if any of the swine are still in this rat-hole."

"Give 'em another bomb first," suggested Ginger. "Stand by, 'ere goes."

The men waited until the reverberations of the explosion had died away; then looked at each other enquiringly.

"Come on," shouted Alderhame, unfixing his bayonet and placing his rifle against the concrete face of the dug-out. Then, borrowing a bomb from the obliging Anderson, he led the way into the underground refuge, while Setley following, closely at his heels, flashed a torch over his comrade's shoulder.

The place reeked vilely of sulphurous smoke. It had been lighted by electricity, but the concussion had shattered the bulbs. The Hun who had hurled the bomb was lying across the fifth step. A

33

little lower down two more were huddled lifeless against the walls. Another, dangerously wounded, raised one hand in a mute appeal for mercy.

"All right, Fritz," said Alderhame. "We won't hurt you any more."

This was apparently the last of the original occupants of the dug-out. For thirty-five steps the two chums descended cautiously, while at some distance behind came Penfold, Anderson and another man being left to guard the entrance in case an over-zealous Tommy took it into his head to throw down a bomb "just for luck."

"Look out!" cautioned Setley. "There's someone still there."

Muttered guttural words and suspicious scuffling confirmed Ralph's statement. The ex-actor made ready to pull out the safety pin of this bomb.

"Surrender!" he shouted, "or I'll blow the crowd of you to Hades."

"Don't," was the reply. "I've got them properly set. I'm an Englishman—a Wheatshire."

"Hurrah!" exclaimed Alderhame, while Setley gave vent to a whoop of surprise and satisfaction, for the voice was that of Sidney Bartlett.

CHAPTER VIII
CUT OFF

"Entering the main room of the spacious dug-out Ralph and his comrades found the place illuminated by a couple of candles that the Huns, with characteristic forethought, had lighted in anticipation of the failure of the electric current.

The place was a combined dormitory and living-room. Against three walls were tiers of bed-boxes, showing that there was accommodation for at least fifty men. Tables and chairs, looted from French houses, occupied most of the floor space. Even though intended for the German rank and file the dug-out, in the matter of comfort and security, was far more habitable and commodious than those of the British troops. It was constructed with a view of lasting, whereas the British dug-outs were of a temporary nature, pending the long-promised and eagerly awaited Great Advance. It was one of the numerous concrete works that the Huns never expected to have to evacuate so long as the war lasted. To their cost they found that British tenacity and courage, backed by the powerful shells supplied

34

by the munition workers at home, were more than a match for German ingenuity and machine-like methods of waging modern war.

Crowded into one corner of the dug-out were eleven Prussians, for the most part sullen and brutal in features and with the fear of death in their bloodshot eyes. Some of them were wounded; all were caked from head to foot with mud and soot.

Armed with a German rifle and bayonet stood Private Bartlett, as proud as a peacock.

"Glad you came," he exclaimed. "I knew things were going all right when these fellows came skeltering for shelter, and still more so when you flung a bomb down the stairs——"

"We didn't," expostulated Alderhame jocularly. "We wouldn't do you such a dirty trick, Sidney. Blame your pal, Ginger."

"He's all right, then?" asked the rescued man.

"And so are you," added Ralph. "Good for promotion."

"'Cause why?"

"I heard you being cross-examined by the Prussian officer and your replies," continued Setley. "Simply had to report to the O.C., you know. Well, what happened afterwards?"

"They knocked me about a bit," declared Bartlett. "Thought I was kidding them, I suppose, but as it was the right way as far as they were concerned they got a bit more civil. Finally, when the bombardment commenced they pushed me down this dug-out. Crikey! I thought the roof was tumbling in every second, and fifty feet below ground at that. Then when the bomb was chucked down the stairs the Huns here knew the game was up. They nearly fell over themselves trying to get me to take them prisoners—and there they are."

"Any way out there?" asked Setley, pointing to a door at the remote end of the underground room.

"Don't know," said Bartlett. "I'll soon see."

He came back with the information that it led only to a smaller room, evidently set apart for non-commissioned officers.

"Good enough," declared Ralph. "We'll leave the prisoners here until we can send them to the advance-cages."

"You our lives save?" enquired a Hun corporal anxiously.

"Yes, if you behave yourselves," said Bartlett. "We won't drop a bomb amongst you as we clear out. That's not the British way, you know."

Collecting the captured rifles and side-arms, the three Wheatshires returned to the open air, where Ginger greeted his restored pal with grim Cockney humour.

"Wot, more of 'em dahn there?" he asked. "S'welp me. 'Ere goes."

Like a terrier after a swarm of rats Anderson was about to plunge down the flight of steps when Bartlett arrested his movements.

"It's no go," he said. "We've promised them quarter."

"After they tried to do the dirty on us," grumbled Ginger, still fumbling with the safety-pin of a bomb. "I'll give 'em quarter—not 'arf."

Sidney barred his way. Setley and Alderhame joined in an attempt to check the ferocious ardour of their comrade. How the dispute might have ended if allowed to continue must remain in doubt, for a heavy shell, landing in the bay of the captured trench, exploded and threw the four men to the ground.

Half buried with debris they extricated themselves, none the worse except for a severe shaking. All thoughts of the dispute were forgotten.

The Wheatshires were occupying the captured section of the trench, the men toiling strenuously to convert the parados into a parapet. A hundred yards to the right the Huns still held their own. A traverse, heavily defended with machine-guns, had proved too great an obstacle to be rushed in a frontal attack. To the rear of the Wheatshires' position was the barbed wire entanglement that had held up the luckless Coalshires; in front the Germans were massing for a gigantic counter-attack, while on the right of the British battalion the Blankshires had been compelled to give ground. Added to this the German guns had got the exact range of the captured section of trenches, while inexplicably the British artillery were putting up a barrage in front of a position where the Huns had made no serious effort to counter-attack.

This error was the result of one of those elements of chance that often win or lose battles. The telephone wires from the observer's post to the battery had been severed, and already three devoted linesmen had lost their lives in heroic efforts to repair the means of communication. A signaller mounted the parapet and attempted to convey the much-needed information to the gunners, but he fell almost immediately, pierced by a dozen machine-gun bullets.

However well the advance was faring elsewhere the grim fact was patent that the Wheatshires were cut off.

The men knew it. They were literally fighting with their backs to the wall—and it is said that a Briton never fights better than in such a position.

"Stick it, men!" shouted the colonel.

The Wheatshires responded with a cheer.

"Reminds a fellow of the winning goal at Yatton Park," remarked Alderhame, as he shoved a fresh clip of cartridges into the magazine of his rifle. "It's getting a bit of a hot corner."

"Garn! It don't beat my old woman on Saturday night," retorted Ginger contemptuously.

The hurricane of hostile shells continued without intermission for the space of nearly ten minutes. The hastily constructed parapet of sand-bags disappeared in clouds of dust and noxious smoke. The men, gasping for breath, clung tenaciously to the side of the trench, except on the left flank where British and German bombers were hurling their missiles with deadly ferocity. Not only in the captured section of the trench, but along the outer lip of the huge mine-crater, the Wheatshires and their supporting battalion doggedly held their ground, despite the pounding of huge shells that several times blew half a dozen men into a state of unrecognizability.

"What the deuce are our guns doing?" was the oft-repeated question, for, although the gigantic messengers of death were still hurtling through the air, the shells were not directed upon the dense columns of German infantry who were slowly following up the barrage set up by their guns.

Then the crash of the exploding shells from the Hun batteries ceased. Only the distant roar of the artillery duel and the sharp bark of the bombs broke the silence. Compared with the titanic thunder of the bombardment the residue of sound was hardly noticeable. It was the signal for the Wheatshires to pull themselves together to withstand the counter-attack.

In dense serried masses the columns of Bavarian infantry advanced. They came on without hesitation, yet in comparative silence, confident that their guns had so pulverized the trenches their Prussian comrades had lost that the charge would be little more than a "walk-over."

"Five hundred yards! Fire!"

From Maxims and Lewis guns, hastily mounted on the battered parapets, from scores, nay, hundreds, of rifles the hail of nickel from the Wheatshires smote the ranks of their opponents. Like a giant receiving a knock-out blow betwixt the eyes, the field-grey masses recoiled, wavered and broke, in spite of the efforts of their officers to check the rout as the men rushed past them.

Ironical cheers greeted the discomfiture of the Bavarians, then the Wheatshires settled down to undergo the renewal of their punishment, for certain it was that the German gunners, exasperated at the check of the infantry, would renew the bombardment with increased violence.

What seemed worse was the fact that several regiments of the enemy had succeeded in working round both flanks. On the left the Huns, still in possession of part of the same trench as the Wheatshires held, were strongly reinforced. The British infantry were now in a dangerous salient, but still they had not given an inch of ground. Nor could reserves be rushed up to strengthen the advanced position, for the comparatively level stretch of ground was completely exposed to machine-gun fire, to say nothing of the formidable barbed wire that the British guns had failed to demolish earlier in the day.

An aeroplane droned overhead at an altitude of less than a thousand feet. By the red, white, and blue concentrated rings on the planes it was recognized as a British machine. In spite of a warm greeting from the anti-aircraft guns, for mushrooms of white smoke was bursting all around it, the biplane circled serenely. Its object was soon apparent, for, like a whirlwind, shells from the British guns commenced to put up a barrage behind the Huns holding the section of trenches on the Wheatshires' left flank.

Simultaneously four indistinct shapes, resembling gigantic tortoises, appeared in view, ambling leisurely towards the uncut wire.

"That's the sort!" commented Ginger Anderson. He could now reasonably risk drinking the remainder of the contents of his water-bottle. "'Ere come the bloomin' Tanks."

CHAPTER IX
THE ADVANCE OF THE TANKS

"Slowly the mechanical mastodons advanced, reeling from side to side as they skirted the edges of the largest shell-craters. Through their multi-coloured sides guns, as yet ominously silent, grinned menacingly. The weapons, moving easily on their mountings, began to search for their objectives.

Through the waist-deep slime the Tanks floundered, displacing tons of mud under the resistless pressure of the broad-flanged endless belts. A shell from a distant German gun burst close alongside one of the steel mammoths, converting the "invisible" colour-scheme into a hideous daub of greenish yellow, but beyond that the H.E. missiles had no effect upon the mobile fortress. Straight from the triple row of barbed wire the Tanks waddled deliberately and remorselessly. The Huns watched their approach with evident concern, so much so that the bombers engaged in a duel with the Wheatshires across the traverse abandoned the task and scurried to their dug-outs. A few, more courageous than their comrades, directed their energies towards hurling their missiles against their uncanny foes. It was like shooting peas at a crocodile.

As matchwood the stout stakes supporting the entanglements snapped under the impact of the leading Tank's snout. Wire, coiling like writhing snakes directly the tension was released, was swept aside as easily as if made of pack thread. Then, lifting its bluff bows, the Tank ambled awkwardly up the parapet of the hostile lines, displacing sand-bags by the score, and finally coming to a standstill, like a steel Bridge of Sighs, across a canal of liquid mud with grey-coated Huns in place of gondolas.

"She's bogged!" yelled Penfold.

"No fear," retorted Alderhame. "She's just having a little rest. See, her wheels aren't moving."

The Tank was making good use of the stop, whether forced or otherwise, for astride of the trench she opened a terrific fire, enfilading the Germans as they crowded, panic-stricken, in the limited space 'twixt parapet and parados.

Up went scores of hands, but in vain. Mingled with those of the Huns who wished to surrender were several "die-hards," who with bullet and bomb tried in vain to find a vulnerable spot in the armour of their titanic antagonist. A few even scaled the side of the Tank and rained savage but ineffectual blows upon it with the butts of their rifles.

The second and third Tanks were now grinding their way through the hostile parapet. One, bridging the trench, landed immediately over the entrance to a dug-out. The reinforced concrete, set upon a mud foundation, was unable to resist the strain of hundreds of tons deadweight. The fore part of the landship sank until its vertical axis was inclined at an angle of forty-five degrees.

"She'll never get out of that," thought Setley, for the mere possibility of that mass of metal extricating itself from the chaos of mud and shattered concrete seemed out of the question. For perhaps five minutes the Tank remained in this ignominious position, the while spitting out flame from the muzzle of her guns, her tractor bands revolving uselessly since they found no resistance in the soft earth.

The wheels ceased to revolve. To outward appearance the

Tank was out of action. Her guns no longer fired, since the Germans had evacuated the trench and were either risking certain death by bolting across the open or else obtaining a doubtful shelter in their dug-outs.

Then the traction bands were restarted, this time in a reverse direction. Slowly the huge mass of metal, disengaging itself from the debris, backed through the passage it had previously cleared in the parapet, and descended the glacis. Choosing another spot, the Tank again crawled forward, this time bridging the trench and disappearing beyond the parados.

All save the first mastodon had now passed the fire-trench. The one that remained did so with a set purpose. While it bridged the trench it was certain death for a Hun to show himself. A few, armed with bombs, did issue from their dug-outs, but caught by a hail of bullets from a machine-gun they ceased to be effective units of the Kaiser's legions.

The colonel of the Wheatshires saw the chance of straightening the line. He knew his men had suffered severely, but the time to rest was not yet. Armed only with a stick the gallant, grey-haired C.O. sprang upon the shell-scarred parados.

"The Wheatshires will advance," he shouted. "Come on, men; we've stuck in this trench quite long enough."

A hoarse shout rose from the parched throats of the indomitable Tommies as the remainder of the battalion leapt out of the trench they had held so stubbornly. In thirty seconds their former shelter was untenanted save for the dead and wounded and a handful of men told off to guard the entrance to the dug-outs that contained prisoners.

"Hang on to the tail of that Tank," shouted Sergeant Ferris to the men of his section. "We'll have our work cut out to settle the Huns who aren't squashed. Don't leave a single Fritz with a rifle in his hand behind you—I've had some."

The sergeant looked a most ferocious object despite his inches, for he was just five feet one and a half. His steel helmet was dented and bespattered with mud. His face was black with dirt thrown up by a shell that exploded less than twenty yards from him. His great coat was torn away at the waist, while one puttee was ripped away entirely. His left wrist was clumsily swathed in first-aid dressings that momentarily threatened to fall off, while to complete the picture a partly dressed goose dangled from his belt.

Ferris had always the resources of an old campaigner. In one of the captured dug-outs he had found the bird, and with the idea

40

that it would "come in handy after the dust-up" he had lashed the goose's legs round his belt.

"Don't think I'm greedy, boys," he shouted. "You'll all stand in later on."

The Germans in the second and third line trenches were fairly trapped. Their own guns were putting up a barrage behind them. Mere "cannon fodder" the defeated infantry received no consideration from their own artillery. The latter, their one idea being to attempt to hold the British attack, were furiously pouring in shells that no troops could hope to pass through in the open.

There was a stubborn resistance offered by the Huns in the second line of trenches, but the Tanks, assisted by the now wildly excited Wheatshires, were not to be denied. With bayonet and bomb the Tommies rushed the defences and made prisoners of the surviving Huns.

There was still plenty of work to be done before the attack was resumed upon the third and last of that section of earthwork. The captured trench had to be consolidated as a matter of precaution, in case the final attack failed.

"Who's got a fag?" enquired Penfold, stopping in the act of transferring a sand-bag from the parapet to the parados. "Hang it all, did you ever see such mud? It's a jolly sight worse than our trenches."

"Here you are," said Ralph, tendering a very soiled cigarette. "Let me give you a hand."

Penfold lighted the cigarette, then, shouldering the heavy sack, descended very cautiously from the fire-step to the floor of the trench. His feet sank into the slime until the mud and water reached to his knees. Vainly he tried to extricate himself. It was not until Setley and Alderhame threw down a couple of pieces of timber as footholds and tugged at their comrade by main force that Penfold was free from the tenacious mud.

It was an even more difficult matter to heave the sand-bag into position. Again Penfold's legs sank ankle deep. Perspiring freely in spite of the cold he struggled to maintain his balance without dropping the sand-bag from his shoulder. In his efforts his steel helmet slipped over his eyes. Still holding on with one hand to his burden he grasped the rim of his "tin hat." As he did so a bullet pinged sharply against the metal head-covering, the glancing blow causing Penfold to stagger and drop the sand-bag. Blood was streaming down his face.

"I always said that steel helmets were a rotten swindle," he exclaimed, then he broke off abruptly and looked dully at his right

41

hand. The middle finger had been completely severed by the bullet.

"Thought it was my head!" he said. "Hanged if I felt this at all."

"You are a lucky bounder, Penfold," declared George Anderson. "It'll get you back to Blighty for a dead cert."

"Thanks, you're welcome to my luck," replied the wounded man as he submitted to the surgical attentions of Setley and Alderhame. "I call it jolly hard lines, just as we are going forward. Now, if this had happened while we were held up in our trenches I wouldn't have minded. Jolly rough luck, I call it."

Just then Sergeant Ferris came bustling along the captured trench.

"Hullo! Copped it?" he enquired laconically.

"Rather," replied Penfold dolefully. "Suppose there's no chance of my having a slice of that goose now?"

"Where is the bird, sergeant?" enquired Alderhame.

Dumfounded the non-com. clapped his hands on his belt. The goose had vanished—all but the legs, that were still fastened to the sergeant's equipment.

"Must 'a' lost it in the charge," decided Ferris. "I'm off back to look for it."

Regardless of the risk he ran the N.C.O. doubled across the shell-pitted ground. In five minutes he was back again, holding what appeared to be a flattened lump of mud.

"Got it!" he exclaimed triumphantly. "Found it in the track of a Tank. Only the head was to be seen, but I managed to hike it clear of the mud."

"Not much of a goose now, sergeant," remarked Ginger.

"True, lad, true; but it'll wash all right while it's boiling. One can't afford to be too particular these times."

CHAPTER X
THE WRECKED LANDSHIP

"Once again the weary yet undaunted Wheatshires braced themselves for another rush. The period of respite over, they had to make an advance upon the third line of German trenches.

Already three of the Tanks, which had been temporarily sheltering in a large mine-crater, were labouring across the open stretch of ground separating the second and third lines. The guns, never silent since the early morning, were now giving vent to a veritable crescendo of hate.

Almost in the centre of the Wheatshires' objective a large brick building stood out clearly against the sky. It was apparently the only one that had escaped the searching attention of the British guns, and with the exception of the roof, the rafters of which were innocent of tiles, was practically intact. It was a two-storied building. The windows on the ground floor were strongly barricaded, while sand-bags had been piled up in front, forming an effective defence against all but the heavier guns.

While the eager infantry were being held in leash the Tanks sauntered onwards, two making for the wire entanglements, which already were badly cut about, while the third floundered straight for the building, although there were no signs that the place was being held by the enemy.

When about twenty yards from the house the Tank seemed to hesitate. It evidently was pondering whether to go straight through the obstruction or waddle past it, until half a dozen machine-guns, that had hitherto been silent, rattled a hail of bullets upon the monster's steel hide.

The Huns had withheld their fire, hoping to catch the British infantry in the open; but the menace of the Tank was too great for their nerves. Without gaining the slightest military advantage they opened out with their machine-guns, and thereby betrayed their presence.

With a rending crash the Tank charged the obstruction. Sand-bags flew right and left, like mud splashed from the wheel of a motor-car; bricks and rafters clattered pellmell as the mass of metal literally ate into the building.

The next instant a mine exploded almost under the Tank. Tons of earth were hurled into the air, mingled with sand-bags and blocks of concrete. When the clouds of dust and smoke had drifted away the Tank was lying on its side, with the upturned tractor bands still revolving like a derelict escalator.

With a loud yell, about fifty of the Wheatshires rushed forward to avenge the trapped mammoth. As they charged across the open bombs and machine-guns took heavy toll. To Setley it seemed like rushing through a hailstorm, with lead, nickel, and fragments of iron in place of frozen rain. Yet, carried away with the heat of combat, he was hardly conscious of the danger until a bursting shell lifted him off his feet and hurled him violently against a heap of displaced sand-bags.

For some seconds he lay still, hardly able to realize his surroundings. Then cautiously he raised his head and took stock of his position.

He was not alone. Lying on the ground close to him were a dozen or more of his comrades either dead or seriously wounded. Three or four others, seemingly unhurt, hugged the mud, in order to escape the tornado of machine-gun fire from the two intact windows of the barricaded building. Amongst these were Alderhame and Anderson. Of the rest of the platoon none was visible, and since the position still remained in the hands of the Huns it was evident that the rush had been swept away by hostile fire.

"What's to be done?" enquired Ralph.

"Dunno," replied Ginger. "You're senior man now, I guess, of what's left of us. Keep down, or they'll lob a bomb into the crowd of us."

"Crowd," thought Setley grimly. Five all told, capable of bearing arms. And he was in charge of the squad. The sense of his new responsibility stiffened his fibre.

"It's no use going back," he soliloquized. "Nor does it seem at all desirable to stick here, Let me see how the land lies."

Cautiously separating two sand-bags, Setley peered through the two-inch gap thus formed between them. Ten yards away and slightly to the right front were the German machine-gunners, their whole attention centred on the trench that had so lately been theirs. Between the wisps of smoke that drifted slowly from the still reeking crater Ralph saw that the Huns had only two machine-guns left intact, and of these only the muzzle and a few inches of the water-jacket were visible. The rest of the weapons were hidden by sand-bags.

"Can you throw a bomb fairly into that emplacement?" asked Ralph, addressing the redoubtable Ginger, who, despite a severe shaking, still retained half a dozen Mills bombs.

"You bet," replied Ginger. "Two afore they knows they're on the way to Kingdom Come."

"All right," continued Setley. "Alderhame, McTurk and I will follow up with the bayonet. We must wipe both crews out. Ready?"

Crouching ready to spring and hurl his deadly missiles the bomber removed the safety-pin. To Setley it seemed an interminable time before he threw one bomb. Four seconds? It seemed like forty before the missile burst with a loud report right in the centre of the over-attentive Huns.

Up sprang the four men, Ginger with another bomb and the rest with rifle and bayonet. Over the sand-bags they leapt, landing

44

upon the bodies of the bombed gunners, scrambled over the intervening debris and made for the second machine-gun.

"Take that, you dirty skunks!" shouted Anderson, launching another bomb. The missile, missing its mark, exploded harmlessly beyond the sand-bag emplacement.

The Germans faced about, and with levelled revolvers defended themselves against the unexpected assailants.

With a rifle-shot Setley brought down one of the men—a big bloated sergeant—and plunged his bayonet into the second. As he did so, he was just conscious of a tingling sensation in his left shoulder. A revolver bullet, fired at practically point-blank range, had seared his flesh. McTurk accounted for the man who had fired that shot and then went down with a ghastly wound in his throat.

As he fell the dying Tommy grasped Setley by the ankles, bringing the lad prostrate upon the ground. Before he could regain his feet Ralph found himself at grips with a tall, slim, bearded Fritz, who in his frenzy attempted to batter in his antagonist's head with the butt of his revolver, notwithstanding that the weapon was still loaded in four chambers.

Guarding his head with his left hand, Setley recovered himself sufficiently to plant a powerful blow with his fist upon the point of the Hun's chin. The man recoiled, dropped his revolver, and raised his hands above his head. As he did so a fragment of shrapnel caught him and stretched him lifeless upon the floor.

Recovering his rifle and bayonet Ralph regained his feet, eager to throw himself again into the fray. But the struggle, as far as the machine-guns' crews were concerned, was over. Ginger Anderson, smothered in mud, was greedily quaffing the contents of a Hun's water-bottle, while Alderhame, leaning against the wall, was methodically wiping the point of his bayonet. Five Germans and the luckless McTurk lay across the captured weapon, while the sixth Hun, attempting to escape, had been shot down by Alderhame as he scrambled out of one of the windows facing the enemy lines.

"We've been an' gone and done it this time," declared Ginger, wiping his mouth with the back of his hand. "An' our chaps 'ave started shelling the place. Only shrapnel up to now; but if they starts throwin' in high explosives up we go in a sort of fiery chariot that ain't at all to my likin'."

"Can't we signal and let them know?" asked Alderhame.

The rattle of shrapnel fragments against the tottering walls gave him his answer. To attempt to show oneself for the purpose of semaphoring meant certain death.

"Look here; we'll make for the crater where the Tank is lying," said Setley. "We'll have to take our chances of getting strafed by the Huns. I'll lead the way!"

"One moment," exclaimed Alderhame, and still leaning against the brickwork he raised his rifle and fired. Before the echoes of the report had died away a heavy body crashed from the gaunt rafters overhead—that of a German observation officer.

"My bird," drawled the ex-actor. "I spotted him about to descend. See, he had his revolver ready. Thought he'd caught us napping. Now, I'm ready."

With their rifles slung across their backs the three Tommies cautiously crawled round the pile of sand-bags and gained the open air. A fragment of shrapnel glanced off Setley's steel helmet, another nicked a piece out of the heel of Alderhame's boot, but without further incident the trio dropped into the crater in which the Tank lay on its side.

The traction band was now motionless. There were no signs that life existed within that massive steel shell. The tail-wheels, which had been raised as the Tank approached the objective that she had failed to surmount, were buckled by the impact of a fragment of flying metal. The futurist colour-designs on her exposed side were scorched and blistered, while the armour-plate was pitted with honourable scars. At an angle of roughly sixty degrees one of her guns projected aimlessly.

"Which is the way in?" enquired Alderhame. "Suppose this is the entrance to the foyer and palm-court?"

He battered the metal door in the after end of the sponson with the butt end of his rifle. It was a risky thing to do, since the crew, if still alive, might think that the Huns were attempting to force their way in.

"Hear anything?" asked Setley.

"Excursions and alarums without," quoth the ex-actor. "Within the silence of the tomb. By Jove! What a reek of petrol!"

A howitzer shell exploding a couple of hundred yards from the crater in which the Tank lay warned the three Wheatshires that the Huns were still fumbling for their objective. With the crash of the detonation the whole fabric of the Tank trembled in spite of its massive bulk and weight.

"She's almost balanced," declared Ralph. "I believe a little power properly applied would set her on her feet again. Let's try."

The three Tommies, using the trunk of a stout sapling as a lever, sought to force the landship into its normal position, but in vain. Their united efforts fell just short of the required power necessary to overcome the difference in trim.

"See any signs of our boys?" enquired Setley.

George crawled up the incline until he could peer over the lip of the crater. The Wheatshires still held the captured trench, but further progress had been "held up" by hostile rifle and machine-gun fire. Overhead the shells from the distant British howitzers screamed incessantly as they pounded the position to which the Huns had fallen back.

A metallic clank made Setley turn his head The door of the Tank opened cautiously and the bronzed features of one of the crew appeared in view. There was a dazed look on the man's face, while his forehead was streaked with caked blood.

"Cheer-o, mate!" sung out the irrepressible Anderson. "Apple-cart upset? We've come to lend a 'and!"

The man began to cough, and scrambling through the narrow doorway collapsed, pointing towards the interior of the stranded monster before losing consciousness.

Resting their rifles against the side of the Tank, Setley and his companions squeezed through the door. Sliding over the obliquely inclined floor, Ralph found himself brought up by the angle formed by it and the curved wall. His steel helmet saved his head from a nasty blow, for the whole space seemed filled with machinery.

"It ain't 'arf dark," commented Ginger, "barging into" the breech-block of a quickfirer. "'Ow about a light? I've got a box of lucifers on me somewhere."

"Do you think you're chief stoker of a crematorium?" asked Alderhame. "The place reeks of petrol, man. A spark and there'll be a terrific explosion."

"Lucky you spoke, mate," rejoined Anderson. "Matches seem to get our family into trouble. My brother, down Enfield way, got a month for 'aving a match on 'im when he went to the munition factory. Blimey, wot's this?"

He stooped; his hands came in contact with a human body, one of five lying tightly packed in one corner of the confined space.

"Don't think they've snuffed it," he continued. "Wot's to be done with 'em, sergeant?"

Ralph, not altogether pleased at having brevet by his comrade, pondered over the situation. If the crew were not dead they would stand a better chance of recovering consciousness in the open air. On the other hand, they would then be exposed to shell-fire, and it was evident that the Germans were getting closer to their objective.

"We'll get them out," he decided. "They'll be fairly sheltered under the lee of the Tank. It's a risk, but that cannot be helped."

With considerable difficulty the three Wheatshires contrived to lift, carry, and drag the unconscious men from the interior of the landship, the task of getting them through the narrow doorway being magnified by the fact that the floor tilted to an enormous degree.

"Nip up and see what's doing," suggested Setley.

On all fours Anderson scaled the side of the crater. In a very short space of time he was back again with his eyes filled with dust thrown up by a howitzer-shell that exploded eighty yards away.

"There's another bloomin' Tank a-comin' this way," he announced.

Greeted by a direct but ineffectual fire from machine-guns and small-arms the oncoming Tank made straight for the mine-crater in which her consort had been trapped. Right upon the very lip of the cavity she stopped. Although her crew were not visible it was soon apparent that they were able to see what was going on, for a voice hailed:

"We'll try and tow you out. Can you take a wire rope?"

"They think we're the Tankers," said Alderhame. "Look here, I'll risk it."

Scrambling up the sloping side of the pit Alderhame, reckless of the shrapnel and rifle bullets, crawled to the rescuing Tank. As he did so two of the crew leapt down, carrying the end of a length of flexible steel wire fitted with a shackle.

"Carry on with t'other end, mate," said one, as he proceeded to fix the shackled end to a massive eyebolt on the underside of the blunt bows. "Think she'll move?"

"You'll hike her up if you pull in that direction," replied the ex-actor, indicating the place with his hand. "She's almost ready to tilt back on her traction-bands."

Without a scratch, although a bullet nicked his shoulder-strap and some fragments of shrapnel glinted off his helmet, Alderhame regained the temporary shelter of the crater, carrying with him the end of the wire rope.

This Setley and Alderhame succeeded in making fast to the overhead girders, although while engaged upon the task Ralph's cheek was cut open by the splay of a bullet that hit the metal-work within nine inches of his head.

"A bit warm up there," commented Ralph, as the two slid to the shelter of the hole.

With a wave of his arm Setley indicated that all was in readiness. Slowly the serviceable Tank went astern. The wire rope tautened, and with hardly any appreciable effort the disabled landship flopped over into her normal position.

"Where's your commanding officer?" shouted the lieutenant in charge of the towing Tank. "Who's the senior man?"

"The officer is unconscious, sir," replied Ralph.

"All right. Shift the hawser aft. Motors intact?"

"I cannot say, sir," answered Setley.

"Then you jolly well ought to," grumbled the lieutenant, who was still under the impression that the three Wheatshires were part of the Tank's crew. "If you can't start 'em up, slip out both clutches. Hurry up we can't stop here to be strafed all day."

Working desperately the three men shifted the wire rope to the required position, placed the crew of the Tank inside, and scrambled in to the interior of the immobile landship.

Setley had a good knowledge of motor-cars and motor-bikes, but the complicated machinery of the Tank was beyond him. Since he was not certain of the way to throw out the clutches, he did the next best thing: he opened the compression taps in the cylinders, so that the pistons were free to move up and down without having to push against a buffer of compressed air.

He was rather sceptical concerning the ability of the towing Tank to drag the crippled consort up the sloping side of the crater, but, to his delight, he found that he was mistaken. Choosing the easiest gradient, the Tank succeeded—not without considerable difficulty—in hauling her disabled sister out of the hole. The appearance of the latter was greeted by a round of cheering from the British infantry and a redoubled dose of "hate" from the infuriated Huns. Not until they were a mile behind their own lines, and sheltered from direct fire by a depression in the ground, did the two Tanks come to a standstill.

"Why, you are Wheatshires!" exclaimed the lieutenant, as Setley and his comrades emerged from the armoured box. "What are you doing here?"

"We got cut off, sir," replied Ralph, saluting. "We saw the Tank in the mine-crater, and we thought we could find cover there."

"And you gave valuable assistance," rejoined the Tank officer, pulling out a notebook. "Give me your names and regimental numbers. It will be a pleasure to me to submit a report upon your gallant conduct in the work of rescue. No, I don't think you'd better try to rejoin your regiment at present. It isn't healthy out in the open. Better wait till after dark."

"By Jove, Alderhame," exclaimed Ralph, after the officer had gone, "if ever I get a chance to serve in a Tank, I'm on!"

"And this bird, too," added Alderhame. "No more foot-slogging infantry for me if there's a chance of riding in an armoured moving fort. Wonder how we could work it?"

CHAPTER XI
AN INTERVIEW WITH THE C.O.

"It was close on midnight when Setley and his two companions rejoined their battalion. Although the distance was not far every foot of the way was beset with perils, for in spite of the heavier fire from the British guns the Germans were systematically searching the ground that had been wrested from them during the day. Every shell hole was now a miniature lake, covered with a thin coating of ice. A slip on the steeply sloping edge and the incautious wight would find himself out of his depth in icy cold water.

The trio met a continuous procession of wounded, most of them having to be carried by their comrades or else on stretchers or sleighs; prisoners, too, who had been humanely kept under cover until darkness fell lest they should be shot down by their own guns, were being herded across the open—gaunt and hungry men who seemed glad to be out of the fighting.

Ration and supply parties, units of ammunition columns passed to and fro, for the firing line had to be fed and provided with bombs and cartridges. Except for the absence of lights the traffic reminded Ralph of the Great North Road on the night of Barnet Fair, with the difference that the predominant colour-scheme was khaki everywhere.

"Hullo, you chaps!" called out a private of the same section, recognizing the three returning Tommies. "Thought you'd been done in. You're marked down as missing. Grub? I've a pannikin on the charcoal fire, and there are some rashers. You've been into the lines of communication? Heard anything of our being relieved?"

"Not a word," rejoined Ralph, taking possession of a thin cup in which the tea leaves from the last drinker were still in evidence. Setley had forgotten to be particular in such matters. "Where's Sergeant Ferris?"

"Blown to bits," said the other nonchalantly. "We didn't get our promised share of goose," he added regretfully. "Suppose we are lucky to get bacon."

The Wheatshires had suffered heavily in the charge. Most of the officers had either been killed or wounded, while forty per cent

50

of the rank and file were out of action. Although they had succeeded in occupying two of the three trenches their failure to reach their objective was galling to the men. Elsewhere the general plan of operations had been successful, and now the battle-worn Wheatshires were consoled with the knowledge that the Huns on their immediate front were in a position that formed a dangerous salient. Either they would have to give back or risk almost certain chance of being surrounded and compelled to surrender.

Dog-tired and bitterly cold, Setley followed the example of his chums and threw himself down on the fire-step to sleep. Shelter in dug-out there was none, for so heavy had been the British bombardment that the remaining shelters were in such a dangerous state that the men were cautioned not to make use of them.

The constant passing of laden men along the narrow trench, the ceaseless roar of heavy guns, and the intermittent rattle of machine-gun fire failed to keep Ralph awake, yet it seemed as if he had been asleep but a few minutes when he was aroused by a hand shaking him roughly by the shoulder.

"Turn out, mate," exclaimed Ginger. "We're being relieved. The bloomin' Downshires are movin' into the trenches."

Setley bestirred himself. Fully equipped he rolled off the fire-step into a foot of mud and slush that formed the floor of the trench. If the Huns had had boards they had vanished—probably smashed to atoms or else covered with debris from the sides of the trench with the violent concussion of the bombardment.

"Wake that man up!" ordered an officer, indicating a dim form. The man was dead, shot in his sleep. Ralph remembered that the unlucky fellow had asked him to move along and give him room. Had Setley not done so the probability was that he would be lying cold and motionless.

Silently the depleted battalion moved along the narrow trench, and with equal caution the goat-skin-clad Downshires filed into the vacated position. It was now snowing heavily, but the Wheatshires paid scant heed to the climatic conditions. They were like schoolboys off for a holiday.

"Hurrah for a good hot bath!" exclaimed Ralph when the men arrived at the rest-billets. In the trenches he had endured cold, dirt, and all the horrors of a confined deep ditch of wet clay with a sort of fatalism; but now the innate desire for cleanliness reasserted itself.

One of four hundred men, all in a state of puris naturalibus, Setley was ordered to double along a narrow plank gangway. Under one arm he carried his uniform. Under the other two bundles, one containing his personal effects, the other his underclothing.

At the end of the gangway were three separate sheds, with a sort of counter across the open doors. As each man passed the first he threw in his uniform, receiving in exchange a metal disc. At the second he parted company with his personal effects, again taking up a metal token. The third but received his underclothing.

Thence the Tommies entered a large building in which were rows of tubs filled with hot water. Laughing, shouting, and cracking jokes the men revelled in the rare luxury, until the stern admonition of the non-com. to "get a move on" reminded them that there is an end to all good things, not omitting bathing parades.

Again the procession was re-formed, and at the double the men hurried along another corridor, passing the other end of the buildings in which their belongings had been deposited.

Each soldier received a change of underclothing at the first hut, his personal gear at the second, and his uniform, steam-cleaned and liberally coated with insect powder at the third. With the regularity of clockwork the battalion was thus furbished up for its stay at the rest-billet—a striking testimony to the efficient organization and to the care and attention given to the troops after their arduous work in the firing line.

"Private Setley!"

The gruff voice of the platoon sergeant brought Ralph to a halt.

"You're wanted at the orderly-room at three p.m.," continued the sergeant. "An' don't you forget it."

"Say, sergeant——"

"Well?"

"Do you know what I'm wanted for?"

"Dunno, me lad; you'll find out when you are told an not a minute before."

Ralph received the message with certain misgivings. The word "orderly-room" had an unpleasant significance. Vainly he racked his brains to try to remember if he had done anything for which he might be "crimed." Then, perhaps, it might be that he was to be detailed for clerical work. Perish the suggestion! He had had enough of that at the bank. He hadn't come out to the Front to follow the irksome routine of doing orderly-room correspondence.

At the hour Ralph reported himself and was brought before the colonel of the Wheatshires.

The C.O. lost no time in coming to the point,

"I've had a report concerning you," he began. "I understand that you were in charge of a small squad, that you rushed a machine-gun emplacement, and that you rendered material assistance under heavy fire to a disabled Tank. The officer making the report states that you behaved with admirable bravery, intelligence, and discretion under highly dangerous circumstances."

The colonel placed the paper on his desk and searched amongst a pile of documents for another. Setley, in the meanwhile, stood rigidly at attention, inwardly ill at ease. He had merely done his duty. The subsequent eulogy from his C.O., although highly gratifying, quite bewildered him.

"Let me see," continued the colonel, glancing over Ralph's "history sheet." "You've served a hundred and fifty-six days with the Colours. You have never been crimed. Your occupation, previous to enlisting, was banking?"

"Yes, sir," replied Ralph.

"Where were you educated?"

Setley told him, mentioning the name of a well-known West-country school. The C.O. nodded approval.

"Wonder why he wants to know that?" thought the lad.

He was not long left in doubt.

"You have been recommended for a commission, Private Setley," resumed the C.O. "I have much pleasure in stating my opinion that you are in every respect fitted to take up commissioned rank. Being recommended, of course, does not necessarily mean that you will get it, but in all probability you will. ...I wish you the best of luck."

"Thank you, sir," replied Ralph.

The colonel made an annotation on the margin of the report.

"In the event of your obtaining this commission," he went on, "have you any particular choice of a regiment? The decision is entirely in the hands of the Army Council, you understand, but as far as practicable the wishes of the individual concerned is taken into consideration."

"Must it be a Line regiment, sir?"

"Unless you have special qualifications for any other branch of the Service."

"I would like to try for the Tank Section, sir."

The colonel raised his bushy eyebrows.

"Dash it all!" he ejaculated. "You aim high, young man. However, since you gained distinction in the Tank affair, perhaps your wishes will be gratified. Meanwhile, if you take my advice you'll keep this matter strictly to yourself as far as your comrades are concerned."

The colonel nodded dismissal. Ralph saluted and left the presence of the commanding officer.

He felt as if he were treading on air. He could hardly realize his good fortune. It seemed like a dream that would be rudely dispelled with the dawn. He wanted to pinch himself to be certain that he was really awake.

On his way back to his billet he encountered Private Anderson looking smarter than he had ever been known before. Ginger's boots shone brightly, despite the "dubbin" under the polish. His buttons, a few hours previously dull and tarnished by the clammy air of the trenches and the chemical effect of the bursting shells, now glittered resplendent in the sunshine. His reddish moustache had been brushed and coaxed into a certain state of subservience, although subduing the stubbly bristles had taken the private almost an hour of hard work. His cap was tilted on the back of his head revealing a well-oiled and studiously arranged "quiff" of fiery-tinted hair.

"Wot cheer, mate!" exclaimed George. "Where 'ave you been?"

"Orderly-room," replied Ralph.

"Blimey, that's where I'm off to," rejoined Anderson. "Your pal the hacter bloke is warned too. It's abart that bloomin' Tank business. Ain't this yere child correct?"

"It is," assented Setley.

"I knowed it," declared Ginger with conviction. "Wot did yer get?"

"The colonel complimented me," replied Ralph tactfully.

"That all? Blow me tight! I was reckonin' on 'aving seven days' special leave an' a free ticket to Blighty an' back."

Ginger walked away, his step a little less jaunty than before.

At tea-time the three comrades met. Ginger was radiant.

"The old man 'e told me I was a bloomin' corporal, and that I was to 'ave the bloomin' D.C.M.," he reported.

"'Any chance of getting back to Blighty on leave just ter show me medal off, sir?' I asked; an' blow me if 'e didn't get the orderly-room sergeant to make me a pass straight away. I'm off to-night, an' chance me arm over them U-boats. 'E's a toff is the colonel."

"And he thought fit to bestow a sergeant's chevrons on your humble," announced Alderhame. "The distinction of the D.C.M. is also thrown in as a makeweight."

"Congratulations, both of you," said Ralph heartily.

"Thanks; and what did you get?" asked Alderhame pointedly.

"'E swears 'e only got complimented," interjected Ginger. "All my bloomin eye, eh, wot?"

Alderhame winked solemnly.

"Give every man thine ear, but few thy voice," he quoted. "I can guess—you lucky young dog!"

CHAPTER XII
"THE BEST OF LUCK"

"A week later Ralph Setley was given his commission and appointed to the Tank Service. He shrewdly suspected that the colonel of the Wheatshires had put in a strong recommendation on his behalf, and in this surmise he was not mistaken.

With the commission ten days' leave was granted to enable the newly fledged subaltern to obtain his kit, and in high spirits Ralph set out for England.

He parted with his former comrades with genuine regret. Despite danger, discomforts, and the rough life he had had a rattling good time in the ranks. Looking back he dwelt only on the bright side of a Tommy's existence. The men of his late platoon were equally hearty and embarrassingly outspoken in their appreciation of Ralph's good luck, because he deserved it. It was not a case of promotion through favouritism: individual merit and devotion to duty had earned a fitting reward.

At Boulogne he alighted in company with hundreds of officers and men, the former clad in "warms," the latter in goatskin coats with the trench mud adhering to their uniforms and boots. All were in high good humour, for were they not bound back to Blighty. A long hospital train had come in, and hale and wounded were cheek by jowl until they set out on the sea-journey—the former by returning transports, the latter in the distinctively painted hospital ships that are occasionally marked down as victims by the recreant and despicable U-boat pirates.

"Hullo, Setley!"

Ralph stopped and turned his head, unable at first to locate the direction from which the hail proceeded.

A man lying on a stretcher resting on the platform had attracted his attention. Ralph failed to recognize the voice, nor could he recognize the speaker. The latter was partly covered with a blanket. His left arm was bandaged, while his head was swathed with dressings to such an extent that only the nose and one eye were visible.

"Hullo, yourself!" replied Setley. "Sorry, but I can't recognize you."

"What, forgotten your old platoon sergeant?" rejoined the wounded man.

"Sergeant Ferris!" exclaimed Ralph. "Why, we were told that you had been done in—blown to bits."

"Not so very far wrong," replied Ferris, as Ralph placed a cigarette between the sergeant's lips and lighted it. "I copped it properly. Lifted off my feet by a shell, then a machine-gun played the deuce. I got in the next night and here I am."

Ferris's brief statement hardly did justice to the man's grit. The calf of the right leg had been pulverized by half a dozen machine-guns bullets, although the shin bone had escaped injury. Two bullets had completely pierced the left ankle. These wounds, combined with shell-shock, rendered the sergeant unconscious. When he came to, the Wheatshires had retired to the captured second line trench and he found himself in the open. Indomitably he started to crawl back. Every inch of the way was fraught with agony. At length he approached a sunken road, but just as he was about to drag himself over the edge a sniper shot him through the chest. At the time he was almost unaware of the fact, except that he felt a sharp twinge, which he put down to a scratch from part of his equipment, but when he gained the sunken lane he again swooned from loss of blood.

Upon regaining consciousness he found that it was night. A burning thirst gripped his throat, and increased his physical torments. Doggedly he began to crawl again, although he could hardly hold his head up clear of the mud. The contents of a water-bottle that had belonged to a dead German revived him considerably, and in spite of frequent rests his progress along the sunken lane was slowly and steadily maintained, until through sheer exhaustion he fell into a fitful sleep.

With daybreak his troubles increased. The Huns begun shelling the sunken road, while the British guns also began to pound the same spot. Crawling into a crater Ferris hugged the muddy earth, expecting every minute to be blown to atoms by the bursting high explosives. It was then that he received a scalp wound and a fragment of shell in his wrist. Throughout the long-drawn day he lay in his frail shelter while the mutual "strafe" continued. At night he resumed his pilgrimage of agony and finally reached the British lines to find that his regiment had been relieved by the Downshires.

"Yes," he continued, puffing contentedly at the cigarette Ralph had given him. "I'm just off to Blighty for a rest cure, then I guess I'll be back in time for the Final Push. Wouldn't miss that for worlds, and the boys are doing great things, I hear. Where are you off to, Setley? Blighty, too. You're mighty lucky to get away. Some chaps have been months out here without having a sniff of home. Got a commission, eh? Well, sir, the best of luck."

Two bearers raised the stretcher and Sergeant Ferris was

borne off on another stage of the journey of pain, yet happy at the thought that a guerdon awaited him—the sight of his native land.

The Cross-Channel passage was accomplished in safety, thanks to the efficient escort provided by the Senior Service, and just as it was getting dark Ralph landed at Folkestone. The train from Charing Cross conveying leave-expired men had just arrived, and the double stream of troops, some with their faces Francewards, others with their backs to the Front for a few brief days, jostled on the landing-stage.

"Blimey, if it ain't young Setley!" exclaimed a well-known voice. "'Ere, Aldy, where are yer?"

And Ginger Anderson gripped Ralph's hand and jerked it like a pump-handle.

"So they let yer off? Lucky blighter! you've got your leave to come. We've 'ad ours, worse luck."

"Cheer-o!" was Alderhame's greeting. "How are things?"

Briefly Ralph explained the nature of his hurried visit home.

"Told you so," said Alderhame. "I knew it meant a pip on your collar. Well, the best of luck."

"Judging by the number of times I've been wished that I ought to have it," rejoined Ralph. "And I believe I was born on a Friday."

"Suppose we ought to salute?" said Ginger.

"I believe the idea is that one salutes the King's uniform, and I haven't got it yet," replied Ralph.

"You salute the uniform not the man," agreed Alderhame.

"Don't know so much abart that," added Ginger reminiscently. "I got seven days C.B. for not saluting my company officer, an' e was in plain clothes; so 'ow abart it? If it's the bloomin' uniform you salutes then why the dooce don't a Tommy kow-tow to every blessed uniform he sees in a tailor's shop?"

"Give it up," declared Sergeant Alderhame. "Well, Ralph, we'll be sorry to lose you, but jolly glad you've pulled off a commission. With the Tanks, too. That's good business. If there's a chance and you're want of a sergeant then you might bear in mind your old pal."

"I won't forget," replied Setley. "So long."

"Shan't be sorry to get across ter France," declared Ginger. "Not that I want ter find myself in those blinkin' trenches: the chap wot swears 'e likes that sort o' life is a bloomin' prevaricator. When we get a move on it's different. But wot I wants ter get across for is a good square bust-out: bully beef an' spuds. Honest, I ain't 'ad me teeth inside a tater the whole time I've bin 'ere. Fed up with Blighty, that's wot I am."

"You're not the only one who had to go without potatoes,"

added Alderhame. "There's an artificial shortage everywhere; those rascally profiteers have been at it again. Just fancy, our little town was quite without spuds, and yet a neighbouring landowner had thirty tons of potatoes under straw—to feed his brothers later on."

"His brothers?" queried Ralph.

"Ay," continued Alderhame, with a laugh. "In other words, his pigs."

The order to "Fall in" ended the interview. The heavily laden Tommies, bent under the weight of their packs and equipment, prepared to embark while Setley made his way to the train.

The next few days passed only too quickly. Hurried visits to the Stores, receiving the congratulations of his numerous acquaintances, modestly relating his adventures to his admiring relatives and going into dozens of personal matters that claimed his attention—these were but a few of the things that occupied the young second-lieutenant's time. The while he was consumed with impatience to take up his new duties. Reports from the Front hinted of important events in the immediate future. Something big was in the air. A "push," long-promised and compared with which the previous operations, magnificent though they were, would be entirely dwarfed, was imminent. At last the British Empire, ever backward in preparation, had more than caught up with her Germanic rival, and with quiet confidence millions of the subjects of King George awaited the news that at last the Huns were being thrown back towards the banks of the Rhine.

CHAPTER XIII
THE BEGINNING OF THE GREATER PUSH

""Haig has occupied Bapaume and Péronne, encountering little opposition."

Such was the news that greeted second-lieutenant Ralph Setley on disembarking at Boulogne. Bapaume and Péronne—places that for months and months had been practically within sight of the British trenches, and yet seemed as far remote as Peru. Miles and miles of deep concrete reinforced earthworks, hundreds of machine-guns, acres of formidable barbed wire, and the pick of the Kaiser's legions, had been in front of those two towns; and yet the Huns had gone—retreated.

"A voluntary retirement, according to our plans." Ralph

smiled when he read the mendacious German official report. Can any sane individual imagine a voluntary retirement in these circumstances. After two years of hard work, fortifying and defending those deep-dug trenches, would any belligerent voluntarily abandon ground gained and maintained at such a cost of blood and treasure?

At a certain place, well behind the lines, Ralph was put through a hurried yet comprehensive "course" in Tank work. In company with half a dozen other young subalterns, he was under instruction from morning to night, with only brief intervals for meals. It would be difficult to find a squad more eager to grasp the intricacies of their future commands. They were, one and all, as "keen as mustard." Technical and practical work, intermixed with lectures on motors, machine-guns and quickfirers, hints on strategy and tactics, map-reading and dynamics—all were drummed into the active brains of the probationers, regardless of the adage, "A little knowledge is a dangerous thing."

"Dangerous for the Boches, let's hope," remarked Danvers, a young second-lieutenant recently transferred from the Air Service, owing to a wound that rendered him unfit to fly, although his capacity in other directions was unimpaired. He had chummed up with Setley, and the two got on admirably. In private life Danvers had been a civil engineer, until the call of the sword took him from the plane-table and theodolite to the sterner profession of war.

"I want to impress upon you fellows," said the major—who acted as instructor—"that you must not run away with the idea that landships are invulnerable."

The class nodded their heads sagely. Considering most of them had seen derelict Tanks—in many cases showing huge rents in their armoured sides, caused by the impact of heavy shells—this announcement seemed superfluous.

"However useful the Tanks have been and are," continued the major, "they have their limitations. They are not perfect. Perfection means finality—and the end is not yet. Landships are a means to an end, nothing more. So don't run away with the idea that you can do anything when in charge of a Tank. It will do a lot. As an adjunct to an infantry attack it is most efficient. When first brought into action landships scored heavily, owing to their novel characteristics. The Huns have now found certain means to counter their offensive, and these means must in turn be negatived. So in the attack exercise discretion until you are astride the enemy trenches. Then you can go for all you're worth. Self-sacrifice is commendable in certain circumstances, but little is gained if you blunder into a pitfall through sheer impetuosity."

Instructor No. 2 adopted a different line.

"Tanks attacking in company," he declared, "should advance straight for their objective and at their maximum speed. Preferably the formation should be en échelon; then, should the leading landship be 'bogged,' the others will have a chance to avoid the pitfall."

Then came the actual practice. Across ground gradually increasing in difficulty the instruction Tanks were taken, first with a qualified hand in charge of each and then with one of the new hands in command. At the end of a few days Ralph was "passed out" as being competent to take a landship into action.

It took two days to bring his command up to the Front. Too heavy and unwieldy to be conveyed by rail the landship squadron lumbered towards the Arras sector, in company with hundreds of guns of all calibres, enormous lorries crammed with shells, and transport of all descriptions laden with munitions and food. Dense columns of marching infantry, regiments in motor waggons, individual units, were swarming everywhere, the Tommies marching with elastic gait and resolute mien, confident that once more the German arms were about to suffer defeat.

"It's Easter Day," observed Danvers, when the Tanks were "parked" for the night and concealed from the prying eyes of a chance hostile airman—the Hun fliers were very chary of late of venturing over the British lines—by means of futurist-painted canvas. "Rummiest Easter I've ever spent. Wonder if the Huns use a similar form of service to ours. Can you imagine the Germans making use of the words of the Litany: 'To have pity upon all prisoners and captives'?"

"From all accounts they are badly using our men who have had the ill-luck to fall into their hands," said Setley. "A platoon of the Chalkshires got cut off, I hear. The men are kept in the German reserve trenches."

"Yes," added another subaltern. "And our fellows are mad about it. The Huns will feel sorry for themselves when the infantry go over the top and get to work with the bayonet. Hullo! the great strafe is commencing."

The artillery fire, constant for the last twenty-four hours, was increasing in violence. The guns of all sizes, from the giant twelve-inch to the fifteen-pounders, were belching forth their hail of devastating projectiles upon the enemy trenches. Vainly the German guns attempted to reply. Literally pulverized by an immensely superior weight of metal, their efforts were hardly of consequence.

"Does a fellow good to see that," observed a grey-haired major, as he watched the incessant glare of the shells bursting in the Hun trenches. "We're top-dog now. I remembered at Ypres we were battered for a week or more and hardly able to reply. Now the boot is on the other foot, and, you fellows, wait till the morning. We've a nice little surprise for Fritz."

There was no sleep that night for the officers and men of the Tanks. All inclination to rest was dispelled by the stupendous violence of the bombardment. The night was rendered as light as day by the incessant flashes, the din was indescribable, while the earth trembled with the crash of the guns.

Rapidly the "dump" diminished, but as fast as the reserve of stacked shells was exhausted more were brought up. The dragon's teeth of ancient Greek mythology were not in it: the projectiles at the disposal of the hardworked but enthusiastic gunners were greater in number as the hours sped. Thanks to the splendid organization of the munition workers at home, the artillery was not in danger of being starved.

"There won't be any work left for us to do," remarked Danvers. "The German trenches must be flattened out by this time."

"You'll soon see," rejoined a lieutenant, consulting his watch. "It's now close on five. The infantry go over the top at the half-hour. Hullo! here's the C.O. It's about time we started."

Already the men had stripped the canvas coverings from the massive mobile fortresses. The roar of the exhausts almost drowned the thunder of the guns. The air reeked with petrol vapour, mingled with the acrid, pungent fumes from the cordite charges from the nearest batteries.

"All correct, sir," replied Ralph's sergeant, as the subaltern scrambled through the narrow armoured door in the afterside of the sponson and gained the complicated interior of the Tank.

Setley gave the word and the mammoth ambled off, fifty yards in the wake of another Tank, three others following at regular intervals. It was still night. Dawn was close at hand, but any indications of the break of day were concealed by the huge clouds of smoke that hung in impenetrable curtains over the German lines. It was snowing. Frozen flakes were whirling through the smoke-laden air. In places the ground was covered to a depth of four or five inches, although everywhere the pure white mantle was rapidly churned into brownish slush by the constant movement of vehicles and men.

Half-past five. To the second the British guns lifted, raining their hail of projectiles on the hostile support trenches and putting up such a tremendous barrage that no living thing could endure in that sector of bursting shells. To those of the high explosive type were added others of a terrible but totally different character. Fritz was being paid back in his own coin and with compound interest. Oft-times the cultured Huns had made use of liquid fire—a hideous barbaric means of attack. Retaliations had been reluctantly decided upon by the British authorities. At last the time-honoured maxim, "an eye for an eye, a tooth for a tooth," was being put into force.

Splendid in their terrible work, the liquid fire shells burst with admirable precision over the crowded reserve trenches. Unable to retreat owing to the barrage, reluctant to face the bombs and bayonets of the British infantry as they kept pace with the lifting artillery fire, the Germans were trapped.

Almost without meeting any resistance the Tommies swarmed over the hostile trenches, and soon a steady, ever-increasing stream of prisoners—men dazed with the horror of the bombardment, hungry, dirty, and devoid of spirit—set in towards the advance cages.

"We're out of it this trip," thought Ralph. "There's nothing for the Tanks to do. By Jove, there is, though! A viper's nest wants flattening out."

CHAPTER XIV
THE COMMAND OF A TANK

"Second-Lieutenant Setley's attention had been directed to a machine-gun emplacement that, notwithstanding the terrific pounding of the Hun lines, had somehow escaped the general demolition. It stood in a slight hollow, the dip in the ground enabling the machine-guns to fire diagonally across the line of advancing troops and, incidentally, into the crowd of demoralized Hun prisoners. Although the arc of fire was limited, the result was hardly less efficacious on that account.

The harmless splaying of bullets upon the Tank's armoured side had drawn Ralph's attention to the source of the hail of small missiles. He could discern the domed tops of the three portable steel cupolas in which the machine-guns were housed. Evidently these metal defence works had been kept in a deep dug-out during the bombardment, and when the British guns lifted had been raised from the bowels of the earth—giving trouble and asking for it.

Round swung the Tank, slowly, ponderously. Her "tail"—the pair of wheels used for steering purposes when on fairly level ground—was tilted clear of the crater-pitted earth. Grimly and remorselessly she set out to squash the viper's nest out of existence.

The Huns held on doggedly. They must have realized that they were already cut off by swarms of British infantry, and that sooner or later they would be "rushed" from all sides. Under the impression that no quarter is accorded to machine-gunners the Boches determined to fight to the last. Even the approach of the Tank, even if it spelt doom, did not make them desert their guns and with uplifted hands shout "Kamerad."

Right and left of the emplacement were lines of barbed wire, many of the posts still standing; but directly in front the entanglement had been flattened, scorched posts and short fragments of twisted wire alone remaining to mark the position. The path for the Tank was invitingly open, but that fact, combined with the determined stand of the Hun machine-gunners, struck Setley as being suspicious. Either the ground in front of the three cupolas was mined, or else a deep pit, with vertical sides, had been dug, and concealed by means of a covering of boards strong enough to bear the weight of a few men but unable to withstand the 200 tons dead weight of a Tank.

With one tractor band grinding ahead and the other reversed the Tank made a half turn in its own length and commenced to cross the front of its objective. Then climbing the rising ground with consummate ease the mammoth charger drew up to the flank of the machine-gunners' lair.

The Huns in the nearest cupola promptly bolted and surrendered to the nearest Tommies they met. Those in the second one, firing to the last, were neatly "done in," for the Tank, charging the metal-box obliquely, toppled it into the nearest mud and finished off by pulverizing the light steel plating and the crew within.

The men belonging to the third machine-gun, seeing that their mobile fortress was powerless against the immensely superior weight of the Tank, fled for the nearest dug-out. Three were shot down by the Tank's machine-gun, while two managed to reach the doubtful shelter. Too late they discovered that the dug-out had caved in under the impact of a huge shell, and only the entrance and a few steps were left.

Ralph ordered his command to be brought to a standstill. His work for the present was accomplished. The rounding-up of the two surviving Huns must be left to the infantry, numbers of whom were swarming over the captured lines, securing prisoners and exploring dug-outs lest the gentle Boches had left explosives with time-fuses in those cavernous depths.

Setley gave a whoop of surprise and delight as a dozen Tommies approached. They were the Wheatshires—his late regiment—and, to be more exact, men of his former platoon. But in vain he looked for Sergeant Alderhame. Penfold—well, he could hardly be expected to be out at the Front so soon. But there was Sidney, the lad with Polish blood in his veins. George Anderson, too.

Ralph felt tempted to shout as the little Cockney dashed past the stationary Tank. With his rifle slung across his back, and a bomb held ready to hurl, Ginger was the personification of activity and alertness. He had spotted the two Huns in the mouth of the dug-out. It would be obviously unwise for Ralph to attract the bomber's attention.

"Up with yer dooks!" shouted Ginger, swinging the bomb.

One of the men obeyed promptly, begging the while for quarter.

"Course you'll save your hide, Fritz," said his conqueror encouragingly. "Mike, take that blighter out of it, will yer?"

Remained one Hun, a tall, broad-shouldered lout, with a face that had animal cunning and ferocity written on every line of it. He stood with his rifle and bayonet at the "ready." His last cartridge had been spent. He was determined to fight to the last.

"Up with 'em!" yelled Ginger, brandishing the Mills bomb, while other men of the platoon gradually closed in upon the solitary Prussian.

The Hun made no attempt to comply. Snarling, he lunged ineffectually at a Wheatshire who had come almost within reach of the glittering steel.

"Hanged if I can do the bloomer in with this," exclaimed Ginger, placing his supply of bombs on the ground and grasping his rifle.

"Form a ring, chums, an' see fair play. Now, Fritz, it's either you or me."

"I haf no chance," replied the Prussian. "If out I come der odders vill shoot in my back."

"Don't talk rot, Dutchy," protested Anderson. "We ain't 'Uns. Either 'ands up or fight me!"

The Prussian had more faith in a British Tommy's word than he had in his own. Still snarling, he emerged cautiously from his retreat; then, finding that no attempt was made on the part of the other men to molest him, he crouched behind his bayonet and stealthily approached the imperturbable Cockney.

With a longer reach and armed with a rifle and bayonet of greater length than the British service weapon the Hun had a certain advantage; but lack of initiative and the slowness of his mental and physical powers neutralized his ascendancy over the short, sturdily built Wheatshire corporal.

Thrice the steel crossed. Once the Prussian's bayonet rasped against the wood casing of Ginger's rifle—a foiled effort to cripple his antagonist's fingers. By a brilliant parry Anderson knocked the point aside, and the next instant his bayonet was thrust deeply into the Hun's body.

"Well done, Ginger!" shouted his comrades.

"Too bloomin' well done," rejoined the victor. "'Ere, you chaps, who's gotter fust-aid dressin'? Mine's been kippered. Thanks, mate."

And almost before the heat of the combat had had time to cool Anderson was on his knees by the side of his late adversary, working diligently to staunch the flow of blood from the wound that he had made.

"Yer asked for it properly, Fritz," he exclaimed. "Why didn't yer put yer bloomin' 'ands up when I told yer?"

In answer, the wounded Hun turned his head and bit the hand of the man who was tending him.

"Yer rotten cannibal!" ejaculated Ginger, and disregarding the advice of his comrades to knock the fellow over the head, Anderson gathered up his bombs, slung his rifle over his shoulder, and vanished from Setley's view.

By this time the battle had rolled onwards. Away on the right German shells were pounding the slopes of Vimy Ridge. That was a good sign. It proved that the British troops had secured a footing in what was unquestionably a key to this section of the hostile line.

Hindenburg had had his wish gratified—to meet the British in the open. He had failed to gain anything by it. In trench warfare the New Army had proved itself superior to the product of the German High Command, and now, with their trenches left miles in the rear, the Tommies were "mopping up" the Huns as neatly as the most exacting commander could wish.

And yet an admirable restraint was noticeable in the movements of the attacking troops. In the heat of the battle and joy of victory it was pardonable for the men to wish to push on beyond the protection of their artillery. With a very few exceptions the various units kept well under control. Never was the maxim "Hasten slowly" better applied.

A motor-cyclist, riding furiously and yet avoiding the yawning shell craters with a dexterity acquired by long practice, pulled up by the side of the stationary Tank. With the engine still running and keeping the machine balanced by placing one foot on the ground, the grimy mud-caked dispatch rider delivered his message.

"There's a Tank bogged fifty yards south-east of Henricourt Farm, sir," he reported. "The CO. sends orders for you to proceed to her assistance."

"Very good," replied Setley, and closing and locking the door, he gave instructions for full speed ahead to the aid of his crippled consort.

CHAPTER XV
THE BOGGED LANDSHIP

"Full speed ahead represented a speed of nearly ten miles an hour, not taking into consideration detours and slowing down to avoid craters and other obstructions. Henricourt Farm, Ralph found by consulting his large scale map, was approximately two miles away, and on the eastern slope of Vimy Ridge. Barring accidents, the Tank ought to be on the spot in fifteen minutes.

Already the motor-cyclist dispatch-rider was speeding over the rough ground on his return journey. Setley could not help admiring the pluck and determination of the man. Not only had he to avoid shell-holes, heaps of debris and stray strands of barbed wire, but the while desultory shells from the German long-distance guns were "watering" the ground in a vain hope of checking the irresistible British advance.

Even as Ralph looked a projectile struck the ground almost under the dispatch-rider's front wheel. With a lurid flash the shell burst, throwing masses of earth in all directions. Through the yellowish-green smoke the subaltern had a momentary glimpse of the motor-bike flying in one direction, the rider in another.

"Gone West, poor fellow," thought Ralph; but almost the next instant the man picked himself up and staggered towards the prostrate machine. The motor-cycle had finished its career. It consisted mostly of a tangled mass of steel and a grotesquely bent petrol tank.

"We'll have that fellow in," said Setley to his sergeant—a

trustworthy non-com. of the name of Archer. "Tell him to look sharp about it."

Although the sergeant shouted at the top of his stentorian voice to the dispatch-rider he paid no attention. Either the roar of the distant guns drowned his words, or else the man had been rendered deaf by the concussion. To remain there in the open was to court death from bullets which were "plonking" sullenly into the sodden earth.

"Shell-shock, sir, that's what it is," declared Sergeant Archer. "I'll fetch him in."

A shell bursting eighty yards away sent fragments rattling harmlessly on the Tank's armoured side. The dispatch-rider never turned his head. It was a clear proof that he had lost his sense of hearing.

Descending from the comparative security of the landship Archer raced across the intervening distance. It was not until he touched the unfortunate man on the shoulder that the latter was aware of his presence. He stared vacantly at the non-com., then pointed to the wreckage of his motor-cycle, but although his lips moved he was unable to utter a sound. It was a bad case of shell-shock. Without sustaining visible injury, he had been deprived of both speech and hearing.

Archer pointed towards the waiting Tank, but the man obstinately shook his head and turned his attention once more to the smashed motor-cycle.

"It's nah-poo!" yelled the non-com. "You come along with me at once."

The vocal effect was completely thrown away, and when Archer gripped the man's arm the dispatch-rider resisted strenuously.

Just then another motor-cyclist dashed up. He was riding with a set purpose, and could not stop to see what was wrong. Crippled motor-bikes were too common objects. Like the Levite, he passed by on the other side.

Close behind came another motor-cyclist He evidently was returning, having accomplished his errand, and was merely indulging in a friendly "speed-burst" with the other man. Slowing down he came to a standstill, and surveyed the wrecked machine.

"What's wrong, chum?" he asked inconsequently.

"He's got shell-shock, and is as obstinate as a mule," declared Archer.

There was method in his obstinacy, for seeing one of his own men the disabled dispatch-rider fumbled in his pouch and produced a sealed envelope.

The new-comer glanced at the address and the endorsement, "Highly urgent!"

"All right, chum; I'll see to it," said the man, and with a flying start he leapt into his saddle and rode furiously away.

A look of satisfaction spread over the face of the speechless motor-cyclist, then, staggering, he fell unconscious into the arms of Sergeant Archer, as a shell whizzing a couple of feet over the non-com.'s head buried itself deep in the ground, fortunately without exploding.

Willing hands relieved the sergeant of his burden and lifted the unconscious soldier into the Tank. A precious three minutes had been lost, but, did Ralph but know it, the retransmission of the dispatch was of far more vital importance than the work of succouring the stranded landship.

But by the time Setley's Tank arrived upon the scene the situation was serious enough. The bogged consort was lying on the floor of a vertical pit twenty feet in depth—a cunningly devised trap right in front of a hitherto masked position, where nearly a hundred of the Prussian Guard, supported by a strong machine-gun detachment, still held out.

Into the pit the Huns were lobbing bombs galore. These did but little damage, although the fumes were trying the crew of the trapped mammoth very severely, and, to make matters worse, the enemy had brought up a liquid flame apparatus from an undemolished dug-out and were about to squirt a fiery stream upon the helpless and hapless Tankers.

In front of the position lay between forty and fifty dead or wounded Highlanders—reserves, who, caught in the open while advancing in support of an Irish battalion, had been surprised and mown down by machine-gun fire. The wily Prussians had lain low when the first wave of British had swept over their trenches, and by one of those inexplicable omissions a detachment had not been left to consolidate and clear up the captured ground.

Several of the wounded Jocks frantically cheered the oncoming Tank, at the same time shouting warnings that there was a pitfall in front. Some of them actually staggered to their feet, and grasping their rifles followed the ponderous landship as it approached the ridge held by the men of the Prussian Guard.

Almost at the brink of the exposed trap Setley brought his command to a halt. While the quickfirers and machine-guns replied most effectually to the Boches' fire the subaltern examined from the interior of the Tank the nature and extent of the barrier that lay betwixt him and the enemy.

The pit measured roughly fifty feet by thirty. A little less than half of the covering still remained—fir planks covered with a few inches of clay that harmonized with the surrounding ground. Unless the Huns had constructed another pitfall alongside this one, it would be practicable to pass it by keeping a few yards to the left.

The roof of the trapped Tank was plainly visible, but there were no signs of any of her crew. In their unenviable position they could do nothing in self-defence. The edge of the pit intervened between the muzzles of the Tank's guns and the hostile trench, but this did not prevent the Huns hurling their bombs over the parapet into the pit.

There was no chance of extricating the snared mastodon. Unlike the one that was towed out of action when Setley, then a mere private, played such a daring part, the Tank was penned in by the four vertical sides of the deep cavity—climbing a vertical wall of stiff clay is one of the accomplishments that a Tank cannot do. Later on, when the foe were cleared away, gangs of men would be set to work to dig an inclined plane, up which the ponderous machine would be able to climb to the open ground.

Heaving a sigh of relief as his command safely negotiated the passage past the hidden end of the obstruction, Ralph steered straight for the strongly held earthwork. The Huns, working fervently to get their diabolical fire-squirting apparatus in order, held their ground. Seeking cover behind sand-bags hastily thrown across the floor of the trench, and crouching in the concreted entrances to their dug-outs, they hailed bullets against the avenging Tank's blunt, armour-plated nose. Bombs, too, burst with an appalling clatter above and below the stupendous moving fortress.

The crew gave good measure in exchange. With their machine-guns spitting venomously and the quickfirers barking loudly the British accounted for numbers of their foes, while the Tank set to work systematically to level the barbed wire and flatten out the parapet of sand-bags.

In their puny rage several of the Huns closed round the Tank. Immune from the fire of her machine-guns they rained blows with axes at her tractor-bands, and even attempted to check the resistless, crushing motion by means of crossbars. All in vain: like a hippopotamus beset with a swarm of flies the Tank continued its dignified progress, levelling all that came in its way; until with the now monotonous cry of "Kamerad," the surviving Prussians surrendered.

"Let a couple of Jocks take 'em back, sir," suggested Sergeant Archer. "All the stuffing's knocked out of them, I guess."

A few slightly wounded Highlanders cheerfully accepted the commission. Thirty badly scared Prussian Guardsmen, deprived of their arms and accoutrements, meekly submitted to be marched off under the escort of the indomitable Scotsmen, while in order to ingratiate themselves with their captors the Huns voluntarily carried several of the British wounded to the advanced dressing stations.

Setley's next task was to render what assistance he could to the crew of the bogged Tank. Already the crew, finding that the mild bombardment with bombs had ceased, had emerged from their metal-box and were somewhat ruefully surveying the unclimbable walls of their prison.

"Hullo, Danvers!" shouted Ralph. "Sorry you've had ill-luck. We'll find a means to haul you out; but your bus must wait, I'm afraid."

Cautiously, and with his revolver ready for instant action, Sergeant Archer, accompanied by two of the crew, descended into a dug-out, the entrance of which was not blocked sufficiently to prevent squeezing through. Within were half a dozen dead Huns— killed instantly by the concussion of a high-explosive shell, yet without a wound on them. Apparently, the dug-out formed the engineers' store, for there were tools in plenty, including mattocks, spades, sectional ladders, and ropes.

Returning with his find, the sergeant was about to report upon his success when a bomb hurtled through the air. Instantly the three men threw themselves flat on their faces, while a second later the missile exploded without doing them harm beyond covering them with mud and dust.

Starting to his feet, Archer levelled his revolver. He was at a loss to discover the whereabouts of the thrower. It seemed as if the missile had been projected from the Tank, until a burst of machine-gun fire leapt from her side into the wall of earth within three feet from the muzzle of the gun.

The landship had come to a stop immediately opposite the mouth of a dug-out which had been so badly battered that the timber props were leaning together like an inverted V. Within a desperate Hun still lurked, and finding Archer and the two men in the open he had hurled a bomb in the hope of strafing the Englishmen.

"Hands up!" shouted Archer, flattening himself against the bank of earth by the entrance of the dug-out and firing a couple of shots into the cavernous recess by way of adding weight to his words.

There was no reply.

"That Maxim laid the blighter out, sergeant," suggested one of the men.

"I won't chance my arm on that," declared Archer. "Hand me that spade."

Removing his steel helmet, the non-com. placed it on the handle of the spade and thrust it carefully in front of the partly blocked tunnel. Again there was no response to the silent invitation. Archer repeated the tactics, this time exposing a little more of his metal head-dress.

A rifle-shot rang out. The helmet was completely perforated by the bullet.

"All right, Fritz," exclaimed the sergeant. "If you won't give in like a sensible fellow we'll have to rout you out. I've a smoke-bomb ready."

"Is that an English officer who speaks?" enquired the lurking German.

"A British sergeant—quite good enough for a Boche to argue with," retorted Archer. "So you speak English? Come out and surrender. That's plain enough, and you know it."

"What's happening, sergeant?" asked Setley, who, screened by the immense bulk of his Tank from the Hun's lair, had been conversing with Danvers.

"There's a Boche in this dug-out, sir," reported the non-com. "Be careful, sir; he chucked a bomb out just now. I believe he's an officer, because he enquired if he was chewing his rag to a British officer."

"I officer am," interposed the unseen. "To you I make surrender."

"Right-o," replied Ralph. "Out you come."

The head and shoulders of a Prussian appeared. Setley stepped forward to receive his prisoner, when with a curse the treacherous Hun hurled a bomb full at the face of the subaltern.

With outstretched hand Archer intercepted the flying missile and hurled it whence it came, where it exploded with a hollow vibration.

"Good thing I'm a cricketer, sir," he remarked. "That ought to have settled the swine's hash. There's no trusting a Prussian."

"Don't," ordered Ralph, as the non-com. was about to investigate. "We'll run no unnecessary risks, but the blighter must be accounted for. Where's a smoke-bomb?"

71

The Prussian officer was still alive. The mention of the word "smoke-bomb" made him find his tongue. He had very strong objections to being driven from his shelter like a rat from its hole. It was he who had ordered the liquid fire apparatus to be brought to play upon the bogged Tank, and now, when threatened with efficacious but comparatively humane measures, he asserted that the British soldiers were taking a mean advantage.

"You've put yourself out of court," exclaimed Setley. "For your treachery you deserve to be exterminated; but we'll give you another chance. Come out and we'll give you quarter. Any attempt at your low-down games and you'll be shot down."

The Hun hesitated. Having no regard for his own plighted word, he had doubts concerning the British officer's pledge.

"I will not surrender make," he shouted almost spluttering in his rage. "This a magazine is. If you a smoke-bomb throw den I fire der powder an' blow you and your landship to pieces."

"We'll risk that," replied Ralph coolly.

The bomb was tossed into the mouth of the dug-out. Nauseating, pungent fumes wafted out. For thirty seconds there was no sign of the Prussian. With their revolvers ready, Ralph and the sergeant crouched by the side of the flattened trench.

Suddenly a grey-coated figure dashed through the asphyxiating smoke. Temporarily blinded by the vapour, well nigh suffocated, the Prussian floundered into the open air, until his bent head came into violent contact with the side of the Tank. Like a felled ox he dropped upon the ground.

"Blessed if he isn't the very image of Little Willie, sir," remarked the sergeant, turning the Prussian over with his boot.

"He certainly looks a mental degenerate," agreed Ralph. "Here, stop those men. Let them carry him in."

A batch of thirty prisoners, under the escort of an imperturbable Tommy, came trudging across the open. They were Saxons; perhaps that accounted for the rough handling they accorded the Prussian officer.

"I've seen the last of that gentleman, I hope," remarked Setley. "You've found a rope? And ladders, too, I see. Look alive there."

Danvers and his men were soon extricated from the pitfall. With them was a German colonel, a tall, sparely built man, who was trembling violently in every limb.

"We hauled him out of a dug-out on our way up," explained Danvers. "The old bus squatted right over the entrance, and this cheerful Hun surrendered. We couldn't send him back. There were no men available for that job. Besides, there was a pretty hot machine-gun fire just then; so we hauled him on board. We hadn't gone a couple of hundred yards when the colonel josser began to get jumpy. He jabbered away as hard as he could, but as I don't understand the beastly Hun jargon I told him to shut up. After all, he was trying to tell me we were blundering into a trap—not out of consideration for us, you understand, but because he didn't relish the big bump. It was his own cowardly carcase of which he was thinking.

"Then came the big bump. Talk about peas in a box. They weren't in it. Thought the Tank was going to turn upside down, but she pitched on her nose with a terrific whump, and then settled down on an even base.

"For nearly an hour the Boches bombed us. At first it was a jolly disconcerting experience, and our Hun started shouting to the bombers to stop it—the skunk! Imagine our fellows doing that. Finding that nothing happened he quieted down a bit, until he suddenly danced up and down regardless of the fact that he was bumping his pig-headed skull against the roof girders. In his raving I caught the word Flammenwerfer several times, so I was forced to come to the unpleasant conclusion that the Huns were going to strafe us with liquid fire. Then your bus rolled up and put the lid on. The rest you know."

CHAPTER XVI
ALDERHAME'S GOOD SHOT

"A barrage of shrapnel put up by the retreating enemy urged upon Setley the necessity for taking cover. There was now no need for further offensive work. The British infantry had occupied sufficient front for them to consolidate. To proceed further before the howitzers and heavy guns could be moved up to cover the advance was injudicious. It could be done. The Tommies, in their enthusiasm, would have pressed on miles ahead, but prudence on the part of the cool and calculating staff officers forbade such a step.

"All aboard," ordered Ralph, and with a double crew, the captured Hun colonel and the shell-shocked dispatch rider in addition, his landship ambled sedately to the rear, making light of the showers of shrapnel bullets that rattled ineffectually upon her metal hide.

Beyond the barrage she passed columns of fresh troops hurrying forward to hold the ground gained, the men cheering the shell-splayed Tank with the greatest enthusiasm. Other columns were overtaken, going in the opposite direction—immense droves of muddy, dejected, hungry Huns and a constant stream of British wounded, some lying motionless upon stretchers, others being supported by their less wounded comrades or else hobbling along unaided save for the assistance of a rifle used as a crutch. Even in their pain the gallant Tommies cheered the returning landship, and exchanged jests with those of the crew who in their exuberance had climbed upon her curved roof.

Guns, too, were going in both directions, the British heavies as fast as gangs of skilled men laid sections of railway lines—the work proceeding at a rate that would astonish even the most hustling Yankee. British horses, too, were making for the rear, dragging captured German artillery, floundering gallantly through the mud as if conscious of sharing in the glory of the day.

Ralph's task was not complete with the "housing" of his Tank under its canvas cover. His report had to be written up and sent in, he had to attend a supplementary tactical conference in order to be acquainted with the general scheme of operations for the morrow. Prisoners had to be interrogated, maps studied—in short, sheer hard mental work following upon a task of hard and arduous activity, until utterly fagged he was glad to snatch a few hours' rest before renewing a close acquaintance with the Huns.

He fell into a deep dreamless slumber, that even the ceaseless thunder of the guns, that hurled their terrible missiles upon the German positions, failed to disturb.

Just after midnight Setley was roused by a hand shaking his shoulder. Sitting up, yet sufficiently cautious to avoid bumping his head against the beams of the dug-out, he found Danvers by the side of the bundle of straw that formed his bed.

"A plane has been strafing us," announced his brother-officer. "'Fraid some of the plums dropped precious close to our buses. Come along and see if there's any damage."

Setley went out, shivering in the cold night air. It was a starless night. The lurid flash of the guns lighted the horizon and threw vague shadows across the crater-pitted ground that a few days previously had been the No Man's Land of the contending forces. It was now three miles to the rear of the advancing British line.

A crowd of officers and men wearing steel helmets and great-coats poured across the ground, all making towards the spot where the Tanks were "parked."

"All right, sir," Setley heard one of the sentries report to the senior major. "They did fall a bit close, sir, but not near enough to do any damage."

"Thank goodness!" ejaculated Ralph, but to satisfy himself he approached the landship under his command. Not even the canvas covering was injured, although two Tanks in the vicinity had had their wrappings torn off by the blast of the exploding bomb.

"The fellow evidently knows where the Tanks are," observed Danvers. "Deucedly funny how these Huns find out things behind our lines, and yet not a single enemy airman has ventured over in daylight for the last week. Eh, what's that?"

A Tommy, hurrying past, had shouted some information to a pal. Halting, he repeated the news to the subaltern, speaking with a grim relish.

"'E dropped two bombs, sir, smack into No. 9 Advance Cage, sir. Never seen such a blessed mess in all me life. I'll allow there are a couple o' hundred prisoners snuffed out. Anyway, they've got something to be thankful for. Their carcases won't be used for pigs' food."

"That knocks your information theory on the head," observed Ralph. "The airman evidently trusted to luck and it played a shabby trick on the prisoners."

"Not at all," said Danvers stoutly. "He was trying for the Tanks. The fact that a cage was within five hundred yards of them didn't trouble him at all. Cannon fodder, you see; once these Huns are prisoners they cease to count in the estimation of the German High Command. That's why it is not advisable to commit reprisals upon prisoners. Such a step wouldn't affect the Huns in the slightest. It's a safe card to bombard their 'open' towns by way of reprisals. That makes them squeal."

"Let's be getting back," suggested Ralph, stifling a yawn.

"Wish I could," rejoined his companion, consulting the luminous dial of his watch. "Unfortunately I'm down for duty at one-thirty."

"What's up, then?" enquired Setley.

"Over there," replied Danvers, pointing towards the front trenches. "They've had a squad from a Labour Battalion hard at it, digging a path for my bus. I was warned to be there at the time I mentioned. Wanted to hang on all the while, but there was that strafed official enquiry."

"I'll go with you," suggested Ralph.

"You're dog tired," objected his chum.

"Not at all," protested Setley. "I'll go. It'll give me an appetite for breakfast, don't you see. I heard that there was to be a variation

75

from the almost everlasting bully beef. There's bacon, Danvers, actually bacon."

"Good!" exclaimed the subaltern. "Let's hope it won't be like the last I tasted. The stuff must have chummed up with the dead end of a poison gas shell. Ugh! It put me off entirely."

"Know the way?" asked Ralph.

"Rather," was the confident reply. "And I guess we won't be lonely. There's plenty of life along the path—and death, too," he added gravely. "We'll follow the track of the Tank."

The well-defined path flattened out by the tractors of Setley's Tank on its return journey afforded a sure guide, although the compressed mud was covered with two or three inches of water. Nevertheless the two officers proceeded with caution; there was no knowing whether a hostile shell or two had pitched after the landship's return, in which case there was a possibility of tumbling into five or six feet of icy-cold water that had drained into the recently formed crater.

"Fritz is still getting badly strafed." observed Danvers, for the guns were thundering unceasingly. The horizon facing the two subalterns was one series of lurid flashes as the British shells pounded the German lines. Haig was taking no unnecessary risks. He was not a leader to needlessly sacrifice his men in costly frontal attacks in close formation. That was a German method of military warfare that had not been accepted by other nations as an essential to success.

There was a certain mistiness in the air. The stars were obscured. The faint breeze hardly disturbed the huge clouds of orange-tinted smoke that stood out clearly against the darkness. Away in the distance a huge conflagration showed that the British shells had set fire to a German "dump," or else the Huns were up to their latest display of kultur—setting fire to a village before "voluntarily retiring to fresh positions."

Contrary to Danvers' expectations their journey was not overburdened with company. The reliefs had gone; the wounded had been carried off. A few "sanitary squads," searching in the darkness, were the only men they met during the first mile of the way.

An aeroplane droned overhead. Neither of the subalterns paid much heed to it. Aviators [unreadable text] night and day were as common as [unreadable text] in the early autumn. Ralph [unreadable text]ver, that it was flying low, its [unreadable text] silhouetted against the glare on the sky-line.

76

"Beastly cold job," remarked Danvers. "All[unreadable text] in summer, but on a night like this——"

"He's planing down," said Setley. "He's shut off his motor."

"So he is," agreed Ralph's companion. "Wonder why? I shouldn't think a fellow would make a landing here for choice."

They plodded on for another two hundred yards. Suddenly a guttural voice shouted, "Wer da?"

"Huns!" whispered Ralph. Both officers drew their revolvers.

"Are you in need of assistance?" asked Setley in German.

"No, but repairs will take two hours," was the reply. Then, after a pause, "How far am I from Douai?"

Setley thought fit to enlighten the Hun, who had evidently lost his bearings in addition to sustaining damage to his machine. By enquiring for Douai, where the Germans had an aviation ground, the Boche had given himself away.

"Quite an impossible distance, Herr Aviatiker," responded Ralph. "Meanwhile, you are our prisoner. Surrender instantly."

Even then the German failed to grasp the significance of the position.

"Surrender yourselves," he retorted, and placing a whistle to his lips he blew three short blasts. "Our patrols will be up at once, Englishmen," he added, "so do not give increasing trouble."

Another airman joined the first—the observer most likely. Dark forms were approaching. These gave the Huns mistaken confidence, for both began blazing away with their revolvers at Setley and his companion, who, dropping on one knee, promptly returned the compliment.

"Hullo!" bawled an unmistakably English voice. "What's the rumpus?"

"German airmen," shouted Ralph in reply.

"Then they're booked," rejoined the speaker.

The disconcerting nature of their blunder completely astounded the lost airmen. Without attempting to set fire to their machine they turned and bolted. Neither of the opposing parties had been hit in the exchange of pistol shots. Revolver firing at sixty yards on a misty night is not conducive to accurate aim, but with a rifle matters are placed on a different footing.

The foremost of the approaching squad let rip. Three flashes and three reports as one stabbed the darkness. One of the fugitives pitched forward on his face; the other stumbled for a dozen yards and then rolled sideways to the ground.

"Well done, Alderhame!" exclaimed Ralph.

"Dash my stars!" ejaculated the ex-actor. "I hardly expected to run across you—'upon the vasty fields of France.'"

"What are you doing here?" asked Setley.

"Ration party, sir," replied Sergeant Alderhame. "We were hurrying along because we were taking a cheese ration up to our chaps. The cheese was lively when we started, so we wanted to get the stuff up before it walked off. There's Ginger Anderson sitting on top of one lot."

The men were all from the Wheatshires. The supplies they were bringing up were conveyed in specially constructed wheelbarrows with broad flanges to enable them to traverse soft ground. Until a narrow gauge tramway was laid down this was the best means of getting rations up to the firing line.

"I'll have a look at our birds, sir," continued Alderhame. "I'm curious to know where they were winged."

"Be careful," cautioned Ralph. "They may be lying doggo."

"Trust me for that, sir," was the rejoinder, then telling his squad to temporarily abandon their highly scented cargo he ordered hem to extend and surround the place where the two airmen had fallen.

The pilot was stone dead, with a bullet-wound through the centre of his back. The observer, hit in the thigh and shoulder, had fainted through loss of blood. "Ripping shot that one of mine!" exclaimed Alderhame enthusiastically. "Jolly rummy, though, I can't help feeling like a sportsman on the moors and it's a human being I've brought down."

"But a bloomin' Boche," added Ginger the materialist. "One the less an' no cause to feed 'im."

By the aid of his electric torch Ralph examined the pockets of the dead pilot, who under his leather coat wore an Iron Cross. Papers found in his possession showed that the two men were crack Hun fliers and had set out purposely with the intention of bombing the Tanks. In addition the disconcerting information was forthcoming that the enemy had learnt the precise spot in which the landships were parked, and since no hostile machines had been over during daylight it was reasonable to conclude a spy had given the news.

"By Jupiter! I'd like to nip the fellow," remarked Danvers, as the two officers resumed their way. "Smart chap that, sergeant."

"One of my old chums in the Wheatshires," said Ralph. "A decent chap, only he has the bad habit of flinging Shakespeare at your head every half minute. I'm rather keen on getting him transferred to the Tank Section, but haven't had the chance to work it yet."

"A handy man behind a machine-gun, I should fancy. Hullo! That was a beauty."

A terrific burst of light, followed by half a dozen minor explosions, occasioned Danver's exclamation. Something, far behind the German lines, had "gone up." The British artillery were doing good work that night.

Floundering past gaping shell-holes, for as they approached the support trenches the craters were more numerous, the two officers arrived at the scene of the Tank's misadventure.

"Getting along famously, sir," announced Danvers' sergeant. "These labour chaps have been slogging in like greased lightning. Another quarter of an hour, sir, and we'll be ready to start."

A great change had taken place in the land topography since the morning. The pitfall lay exposed in all its nakedness—a wide yawning cavity of which three sides were as steep and smooth as a concrete-faced wall. The third had been attacked by the labour troops—picked navvies of magnificent physique and thoroughly skilled in the art of digging.

Earth had been cut away until a slope of thirty degrees formed an inclined plane from the normal surface to the floor of the pit. The finishing touches were being made, thick planks being put down to form a corduroy road up the newly made path.

Members of the Tank's crew had also been hard at work fitting new treads to parts of the tractor bands. Considering the fall the heavy mass had come off lightly, for the injury to the wheels was the only material damage.

Danvers surveyed his command with great satisfaction.

"I'm quite attached to the old bus," he confided to Ralph. "Of course they would have given me another if this one had been properly strafed, but it's simply great to get her into working order again."

"All ready, sir," reported the sergeant. The two officers entered the steel box. The motors were purring gently and rhythmically. Amid the cheers of the excavating squad the Tank moved slowly yet surely up the incline, and, gaining the shell-pitted ground, waddled sedately for her base.

"Now for a few hours' sleep," said Danvers.

Ralph stifled a yarn.

"Yes," he admitted, glancing at his wristwatch. "It's now ten minutes past three—we've done pretty well. At five we start our day's work, and from all accounts it's going to be a hot time."

CHAPTER XVII
THE SPY

"Contrary to Setley's surmise the following day passed quietly—if the term can be applied to operations on the Western Front.

"Nothing of consequence to report," was the official communiqué, but throughout the day the British guns thundered upon the Hun defences. The Germans, expecting a renewed assault, were on thorns; they were so badly hustled that they could not be urged to make a counter-attack. Their reserves were not forthcoming owing to the efficient barrage behind the lines.

Meanwhile the British infantry rested, consolidating their ground and relying upon the artillery to pave the way for the assault when the latter did take place. There are limits even to the endurance of a Tommy, and although the men had the spirit to advance their leaders realized that to attain the best results the operations must be the festina lente order.

So with the infantry inactive the Tanks likewise had to "stand off," and Ralph was fortunate in making up arrears of sleep. At three in the afternoon Second-Lieutenant Setley was summoned to the presence of his commanding officer.

"We're having a shuffle round," began the latter without needless preamble. "Six additional Tanks are being sent up from the Base, and some of the men who have had practical experience in action are to be distributed amongst the crews of the new arrivals. That, naturally, causes vacancies in the complements of the Tanks here already. You sent in an application, I see, for two N.C.O.'s of the Wheatshires. The C.O. of the Wheatshires raises no objections, Headquarters approves, and the men are warned to join as soon as possible. I presume you would like to have them with you?"

"Yes, sir," replied Ralph. "At the same time I should be sorry to lose Sergeant Archer. He's a smart, hard-working, conscientious N.C.O.——"

"I know," interrupted the C.O. "You need not have any qualms concerning Sergeant Archer. He is to be sent on promotion to the Ancre. Very well, then; that's settled. Good afternoon."

Ralph saluted, and withdrew, mentally declaring that the brusque C.O. was a thorough sport. Before he had gone a hundred yards he encountered Sergeant Alderhame and Corporal Anderson, who had just reported themselves at Divisional Headquarters.

"You haven't lost much time," was Setley's greeting.

"Rather not," replied Alderhame.

"He was off like greased lightning, sir," added Ginger, "in case they changed their blessed minds. I'm fair bustin' for a joy-ride in one of them Tanks."

"You'll have your wish, then," said Ralph. "We are shifting tonight. That airman you shot, Alderhame, tried to bomb us last night, and the inference is that the Huns had been told of the locality of the Tanks by a spy. So to avoid further risks we were going some four miles away—somewhere between Givenchy and Souchez."

"That means business," said Alderhame. "We heard that our next thrust is to be directed against Lens. My word! I can see us climbing Hill 70 in a Tank."

"Let's 'ope we don't drop down a bloomin' coal-pit," said Ginger. "I've 'eard as 'ow some of 'em are 'arf a mile deep."

As soon as darkness set in the Tank Division, comprising twelve landships and the travelling workshops and store lorries, proceeded to its new destination, making a wide detour well behind the lines. The new site had been carefully selected; piquets were posted to prevent unauthorized persons approaching within four hundred yards and every possible precaution taken to safeguard the mobile fortresses.

"Quite a fine evening for a stroll," remarked Danvers, just as the hour of midnight was approaching.

"Eh? What's the game?" enquired Ralph curiously.

His chum had recently returned from visiting the outlying posts. In ordinary circumstances Danvers would be able to "stand off" until five.

"Merely a whim of mine, I suppose," he replied. "At any rate, I'm going, but, of course, if you——"

"I'm on," agreed Setley, buckling on his belt, to which was attached his revolver-holster. "Where do you propose making for?"

"Along the Givenchy road," announced Danvers. "It's quite quiet. I've a wish to explore a certain spot a little way off the high road. Ready?"

The way was rough in spite of the urgent and ceaseless attentions of the pioneers. Constant motor traffic had cut deep ruts into the soft ground bordering the strip of pavé. Of the avenue that formerly fringed the road only a few trees were standing. Of the others isolated shell-scarred stumps remained, but for the most part the trees had been bodily uprooted by the titanic blows of bursting explosives. Here and there a dead horse, its stiffened legs sticking up in the air at various angles, showed up in the pale starlight. The Huns had been shelling the wood during the day, and the transport had paid toll. Shattered waggons and limbers, dragged to one side, also bore silent testimony to the work of carnage.

"'Alt!" hissed a voice, and from the shadow of a tottering wall a khaki-clad sentry appeared. The dully glinting tip of his bayonet hovering within an inch or so of Setley's chest brought both officers up with the utmost alacrity. They realized that it was unhealthy to ignore a peremptory order of that description when on active service.

Danvers gave the countersign. The sentry, who belonged to the Tank Section, recovered his rifle.

"All right, sir," he said. "You may pass."

"Everything correct?" enquired Danvers.

"Quite, sir," replied the man.

A quarter of a mile further on the two subalterns struck the main road, along which a constant stream of troops and vehicles were passing.

"Only a few yards of this," remarked Danvers. "We turn off to the left again. See that building—or the remains of one?"

He indicated the gaunt gables of a farmhouse. The roof had entirely disappeared. Not even a rafter remained. The front wall had been blown out, leaving a far-flung mass of debris; the back wall was still standing, although pierced through and through in a dozen places.

"Carefully, now," whispered Danvers. "While I was visiting rounds I spotted someone making for this house. Kept him under observation with my night-glasses. I waited nearly twenty minutes and he didn't show up again. That is in itself suspicious. I would have sent out a piquet, only there was too much risk of the men giving themselves away. It's a task best tackled by us, I imagine. You work round by the right; I'll go to the left. If the fellow is still there, well and good. We'll soon find out his business. If he isn't, we'll wait and see if he returns."

The two officers separated. Keeping close to the ground and taking advantage of a slight natural dip in the untilled field, Ralph approached his objective. Presently he stopped and listened. He could hear a voice either muttering or else expostulating in a sort of jibberish unintelligible jumble.

"Not English, nor French—nor German," declared Setley. "Flemish perhaps, but hardly likely. There's only one man, I should imagine; but why does he carry on in this excited fashion?"

Drawing his revolver, Ralph continued his approach. Cover there was now none. He had to cross twenty yards of open ground before he gained the shadow of one of the gabled walls. In spite of his caution, his boots squelched loudly in the tenacious mud. It seemed impossible that anyone on the alert could help hearing him.

The muttering ceased. Ralph stopped dead. Had the mysterious individual an inkling of danger? For a long-drawn half-minute Setley waited, his feet sinking slowly and surely into the slime. Then the flow of incoherent words was resumed.

Gaining the shelter of a wall, Setley paused. There were no signs of Danvers. He decided to wait until his companion put in an appearance; not that he was unable to tackle the suspect single-handed—there was that predominating factor, his revolver. But, since he wished to take the man alive, he resolved to leave nothing to chance and await assistance.

Peering over the jagged edge of a hole in the brickwork Ralph saw the object of his quest. On the mound of stones that at one time comprised the farmhouse floor lay two scorched beams. On these a door had been placed so as to form a rough table, and spread out upon this was a coloured plan, illuminated by the shaded gleam of a military map-reading lamp.

Bending over the plan was a tall, burly man, dressed in the uniform of a British infantry officer. His face was in darkness, and whether young or middle-aged Ralph was unable to determine.

On the floor by the side of the suspect lay a folded garment—a cloak apparently—and a German army revolver; while to keep the edges of the plan from being disturbed by the wind the man had made use of four clips of cartridges as weights. By the brass material of the clips Ralph knew that they were not British but German.

"Cool cheek," thought Setley. "Quite enough evidence to place him in front of a firing party. He looks a tough customer, too." Presently Danvers crawled up and also took stock of the suspect. The two subalterns glanced at each other meaningly and nodded. Then, bounding swiftly and agilely through the gap in the wall, they threw themselves upon their quarry.

The improvised table flew one way; the spy, in the grip of his assailants, the other. The plan coiled up and rolled across the rough floor until it quivered against a projecting slab of stone. The lamp, still alight, slipped to the ground, its rays directed skywards like a miniature searchlight.

The fellow put up a tough fight. More than once he shook off his attackers, but was unable to regain his feet and follow up the advantage. He fought cleanly. He did not bite or kick—which was remarkable for a Hun—but used his fists with good effect, as Danvers had cause to know.

At length the two chums gained the mastery, although at the end of the struggle they were almost played out.

"Now what's to be done?" gasped Ralph, when the suspect was securely bound—wrists and ankles—by means of handkerchiefs and the man's own revolver lanyard. "If we've got to bring him out of this we'll have trouble. He's a lump of a chap."

"Get a man to mount guard over him until we can fetch the piquet," decided Danvers, wiping the perspiration from his forehead. "By Jove! My nose feels as big as a turnip."

"It's certainly swelling some," remarked Setley, surveying his chum's features by the aid of the captured electric lamp. "All right; you stand by and I'll bring a Tommy back to look after the blighter."

In less than twenty minutes Ralph returned, accompanied by a corporal of the Tank section whom he had met on the road.

"I've been trying to question the chap," reported Danvers. "Tried him in German. Perhaps my rendering was so atrocious that he couldn't understand, or else he's sullen. He tried to wriggle while you were away, but he seems to be lashed up tight enough."

"Mount guard over him, corporal," ordered Ralph. "If he tries any of his capers prod him in the stomach with your bayonet. I don't think that would be bringing His Majesty's uniform into contempt. We'll take that revolver and the map with us as evidence."

Leaving the corporal furtively eyeing his charge, like a terrier watching a rat, the two subalterns hurried back to the camp.

Having made their report an armed piquet was sent out, together with a couple of stretcher-bearers, in case the prisoner refused to walk.

"I feel rather 'bucked' over this business," remarked Danvers. "Despite a bang on the proboscis, I am inclined to assert that this night's work hasn't been thrown away. I was——"

A rifle-shot rang out, clearly audible above the rumble of distant guns.

"By Jove!" ejaculated Ralph. "Corporal Rogers has plugged the chap."

"Rather a wide interpretation of your orders, old boy," replied Danvers. "Why didn't he use cold steel?"

With the piquet hurrying at their heels the two officers ran across the intervening stretch of mud and reached the ruins. The spy was still there, very much alive. Over him stood the corporal. An empty cartridge case on the floor and the reek of cordite fumes were silent evidence to the identity of the man who fired the shot.

"All correct here, sir," reported Corporal Rogers. "I heard footsteps, went to the broken window, and saw a bloke sneaking up towards the building. I challenged, and he turned tail. Then I let rip, and he dropped. I'll swear I plugged him, but he made no noise when he fell."

Proceeding in the direction indicated by the corporal, Setley and Danvers found the lifeless body of a man dressed as a French peasant. There was nothing on him to prove his identity. Close by, and evidently dropped as he fell, was a small bag of corn. A couple of yards further away was found a little bottle containing water.

"Jolly fishy," declared Danvers. "Corn and water—too small to be of much use for human consumption. What does it mean?"

Nothing more could be done as far as the slain peasant was concerned. The officers returned to the ruins while the captive was being strapped to the stretcher—a task that took the united efforts of four of the piquet.

"This chap's a spy, that's a dead cert.," continued Danvers. "The other fellow is an accomplice and brings him grub."

"But you said that the quantity was insufficient," protested Ralph. "Your theory doesn't hold good."

"Hanged if it does," admitted Danvers, "It's a regular mystery. No doubt——"

A gentle cooing above their heads caused the men to look up. Flashing the light they discovered that nesting in a niche in the end wall was a birdcage. It must have been placed there since the building was partly demolished by shell-fire.

Standing on another man's shoulder one of the piquet handed down the cage. Within were four carrier pigeons.

"The chain of evidence is complete," declared Danvers. "Bring those birds along—and this one, too," he added, indicating the still struggling prisoner.

"A very good night's work," commented the C.O., when the two subalterns had made their report. "Two birds with one stone, by Jove! All right, carry on; we'll have this gentleman tried by court-martial in the morning."

CHAPTER XVIII
THE STRUGGLE FOR NEANCOURT VILLAGE

""Thank your lucky stars that you fellows aren't in Blighty," was the greeting Setley and Danvers received on the following morning, when they put in an appearance in the building pretentiously styled the Mess.

"What's wrong now?" asked Danvers. "Rotten news in the papers?"

"We were referring to your escapade last night," continued the speaker. "Your efforts are like the padre's egg: good in parts. We don't deny that the fellow who was shot by the sentry was a spy, but the other——"

"What about him?" enquired Ralph impatiently.

"Don't jump down my throat, old chap," was the feigned indignant protest. "That's the secret of the whole business. You simply leap at erroneous conclusions like a bull at a gate. Sometimes the gate goes, sometimes it doesn't, and then the animal is sorry for itself. Do you remember what Gladstone said in 'sixty-eight?"

"Nothing to do with this spy business, I'll swear," interrupted Danvers, seizing his tormentor by the scruff of the neck. "Now, you prevaricating blighter, out with it! What are you hinting at?"

"I was testing your knowledge of political history before enlightening you——"

The young officer had no further opportunity in that direction, for Setley gripped him by the heels and Danvers by the shoulders. Between them they bumped their victim till he yelled for mercy.

"Then straight to the point," declared Danvers, "or we'll strafe you again."

"I was recalling the Prime Minister's immortal quotation in the year of grace eighteen hundred and sixty-eight," gurgled the captive, whereat the bumping process proceeded, until the entry of the senior major restored things to their normal state.

"Yes," he remarked, when Danvers had informed him of the reason for the impromptu "rag." "You fellows have made a mess of part of the business. The man in British uniform is a major of the Coalshires. He is suffering from shell-shock, and is now under the doctor's care. Memory gone, and all that sort of thing. Got out of touch with his battalion and wandered into the ruined farmhouse for shelter. The plan he apparently took from a German prisoner, and although in the major's present mental state it conveys nothing to him it means a lot of precious information to us. It appears to be an accurate and official plan of the system of trenches surrounding the Von der Golz Redoubt and the fortress village of Néancourt."

"That's good, sir," remarked Danvers.

"I agree, and so does the C.O. In any case, the plan will enable the C.O. to communicate accurate information to the Brigade

Headquarters, in which event be prepared for the fall of the hitherto impregnable Von der Golz Redoubt."

Outside Ralph encountered Sergeant Alderhame, who was busily engaged in dismantling a machine-gun.

"You might have got me to chip in last night's affair, sir," he said reproachfully.

"Couldn't be helped," replied Setley. "I would have done so, if possible. How do you like your new job?"

"Absolutely top-hole," declared the ex-actor enthusiastically. "I am just pining to have another slap at the Boches, this time inside one of these beauties."

And he indicated the array of landships, now quiescent, like Behemoths resting after a fray.

"You are getting quite vindictive," declared Ralph.

"I came out here with the idea that a German was a human being like ourselves," said Alderhame. "I have altered my opinion since then. Why, only this morning I met one of the Wheatshires back from out there. The wanton damage those brutes did before evacuating some of the villages shows that he is a beast. What puzzles me is that the German Staff isn't afraid of the consequences. They must know they're being beaten. I suppose it's a case of:

"Before the curing of a strange disease,
Even in the instant of repair and health,
The fit is strongest; evils that take leave,
On their departure most of all show evil."

"And I hope you're right," said Ralph. "There seems no doubt that the Huns are getting properly whacked. It'll be a tough job for some time, but they're on the down grade."

"To quote the bard again:
He that stands upon a slippery place
Makes nice of no vile hold to stay him up.

You know, Mr. Setley, since I've been out here I firmly believe that Will Shakespeare must have foreseen this business. How appropriate many of his quotations are! However, quoting Shakespeare won't get this blessed machine-gun re-assembled, so here goes.

Before the day was out persistent rumours passed from man to man that the Great Push was to attain its culminating point—or, at least, a terrific intensity—on the following Monday. The guns had allowed the enemy no rest. On a front of twenty miles tons and tons of shells were being pumped into the Hun lines. It was a bombardment that presaged an infantry advance on a large scale, and that meant that the Tanks were to play a conspicuous part.

On the evening prior to the longed-for day rumour gave place to certainty. The advance was definitely fixed. Come storm or sunshine, mud or dust, the khaki-clad infantry were to go over the top at the hour of five-thirty. Every available Tank was to cooperate; once the positions were won the Tank commanders were to exercise their discretion in pushing on, keeping within the limits and following up the British artillery barrage.

At the final conference, the officers of the Tank Division pored over their maps and listened to elaborate but simply explained instructions from the C.O. The principle objective during the first phase of the advance was the Von der Golz Redoubt. The most practicable means of approach was pointed out—a circuitous route that first meant the occupation of the nest of fortified ruins that at one time formed the village of Néancourt.

"Gain that, gentlemen," concluded the C.O., "and your raison d'être is achieved. Afterwards you can rely upon your own judgment."

Setley, like many others, sat up late that night. There was much to be done on the eve of the battle. He had done it many times before, but there was always the same sort of ritual to be undertaken in case he "went West." The frequency with which he got his personal belongings together, and wrote a farewell letter home, to be forwarded in the event of anything happening, was becoming monotonous. He dreaded the preliminaries, although he knew that the moment the order for advance was received and the Tank set in motion all fears on that score would be flung to the winds and absorbed by the exhilaration of the battle.

The morning broke grey and misty. With the first signs of dawn the infantry stood to arms, clustered as closely as the narrow width of the trenches permitted. Overhead the British shells flew as thick as hail, dropping with admirable precision upon the expanse of tortured earth that recently had been the latest word in the system of German field fortifications. Néancourt village remained fairly intact, as far as observation from the British lines showed, while dominating it was the strongly held Von der Golz Redoubt, formidable in spite of the hammering it had received for the last forty-eight hours.

For good reasons, these two places had not been subjected to a bombardment from H.E. shells. So long as they remained free from the attentions of that sort of missile, the Germans kept their garrisons up to full strength. They held the positions tenaciously, and reckless of loss of life. Since every Hun put out of action meant an irreparable loss to their reserves, it was better for the British to

88

leave a veritable death trap for their foes until the critical moment of the advance than to pulverize the place and thus release German troops for work in more extended positions.

"Those fellows will put up a stiff fight," remarked Danvers, as he walked with Setley towards the waiting Tanks. "Prussian Guard and Bavarian infantry: that's what we have in front of us. I hear that the Saxons and Badeners have been withdrawn. They surrender too freely to please old Hinder-beggar."

"Those blighters are obviously fed-up," agreed Ralph. "Sergeant Alderhame showed me a card he had picked up in a captured dug-out. I have it somewhere—yes, here it is."

He handed Danvers a piece of pasteboard, about four inches by three. On it in German characters was the following:—

"Yield yourself prisoner: any one can who wishes to do so. Clear out of your path those who lead you to the slaughter-house— they alone are your enemies. Think of your dear ones. Do not sacrifice yourselves for princes and the money bags of Prussia. Help yourselves and God will help you.—Hans von Rippach."

"That shows the way the wind blows in the South German principalities," commented Danvers. "Imagine our Tommies passing round a thing like that. Hullo, there's the signal! S'long, old chap, and the best of luck."

Five minutes later the array of Tanks ambled leisurely towards the first-line trenches. Hardly a hostile shell came near them; the few that did were "duds." Not only was the German fire diminished by the British artillery, but the few missiles they did send over were obviously deficient in quality.

Guided by the prearranged signals, the landships made for a part of the British trenches that had already been cleared in order to allow the mastodons to crawl over. As Ralph's Tank ground her way across the deep and narrow trench the subaltern had a momentary glimpse of a close line of steel-helmeted infantry, standing with one foot on the fire-step and with their bayonets fixed, awaiting the shrill blast of the whistles.

Fifty—a hundred yards ahead the Tanks went, greeted by a fierce yet ineffectual fire from scores of machine-guns. Despite the heavy bombardment, the Huns had again managed to keep a large proportion of these deadly weapons intact. Against infantry their scythe-like hail of bullets would be terribly effective. The Tanks, drawing the fire, made it possible for the men to charge without excessive losses.

Straight towards Néancourt village the squadron of landships advanced, but only to a certain point. Then, amid the yells of the

89

exasperated Prussians, who had been hoping that the mammoth steel-clad machines would blunder into a series of pitfalls, the Tanks turned abruptly to the right and parallel to the hostile lines. Thanks to the plan that Danvers and Setley had taken from the supposed spy, the landships were able to attack effectively and without danger of being "bogged."

Within the confined space of the Tank the noise of the motors and rapid bark of the quickfirers and the metallic rattle of the maxims muffled all other sounds from without; yet Ralph caught the sudden roar of the inimitable British cheer as the Tommies swarmed over the top.

It was a case of concentrating all his attention on the enemy. Every hostile machine-gun put out of action meant greater security to the British infantry, and nobly Setley went about his task. Following the Tank next ahead he kept within fifty yards of the enemy lines, the nearest that the Tanks could approach without toppling over into cunningly concealed pitfalls. As hard as the gunners could open and snap to the metal breech-blocks, as rapidly as the maxims could use up their belts of ammunition, the Tank, like her consorts, poured shot and shell into every possible spot that might be a German machine-gun emplacement.

The Huns stood their ground. The terror that had seized them when first they had seen what they took to be supernatural monsters was no longer manifest. They knew what Tanks were, what damage they could do, and that, like other engines of war, they were vulnerable. The fact that a long, deep, covered pit lay between them and the oncoming landships gave them confidence—a confidence that was to be shattered when they realized that somehow the British had learned the secret of the hidden anti-Tank defences.

Again turning abruptly, this time to the left, the array of landships lurched and sidled over the partly flattened-out trench, almost simultaneously with the leading platoon of the charging infantry.

Although the foremost line was thinly held the Huns fought with a desperate and ferocious courage. They were Prussians, steeped in the belief that they are the finest troops in the world, and taught to despise the amateur army that had, Phoenix-like, arisen from the ashes of the "contemptible" little British expeditionary force that, outgunned and outnumbered, ought to have been wiped out by the German legions on the glorious retirement from Mons. Yet it had not. The Prussian military machine had not reckoned

90

upon one thing—the dauntless bravery and stolid tenacity of the individual British soldier.

With bomb, rifle and bayonet, the Huns sought to defend themselves against the irresistible khaki-clad boys. Hardly once was the recreant cry of "Kamerad" raised. In five minutes the British troops were in indisputable possession of the first-line trenches. Here they paused for a well-needed "breather," while the Tanks cleared a path to the outskirts of Néancourt.

Three landships undertook this part of the operations. Others were executing a "turning movement" against the Von der Golz Redoubt. Two were already out of action—one receiving a direct hit from a 5-inch shell, the other toppling over into a concealed pit.

Fierce as had been the struggle for the Hun front trench the fight for Néancourt excelled it in savagery and tenacity. Setley soon had evidences of the desperate courage of the Prussian Guard, for on approaching the barricade at the outskirts of the village scores of Germans boldly quitted shelter and attacked the Tank with bombs. It was a futile, inane act, but characteristic of the temper of the Boches. In a trice the roof of the Tank was swarming with men who endeavoured to find a vulnerable joint in the massive armour. They even rained blows on the muzzles of the quickfirers and tried to jam the tractor-bands by means of crowbars and wedges, while in their mad excitement many were killed and injured by bombs hurled by their compatriots.

Ralph gave orders for the motors to be reversed. With the sudden change of motion the Huns on the roof rolled off like ninepins. Many were caught and crushed under the broad-flanged tractor-bands, others formed an easy mark for machine-guns; while the Tank, shaking herself clear, like a retriever emerging from the water, forged ahead again for the barrier thrown across the street.

It was a formidable obstacle. Trees had been felled so that their trunks—some of which were two feet in diameter—lay athwart the road. Before and behind these were piled sand-bags, stopped with a veritable forest of criss-crossed barbed wire. Between the tree-trunks were two studded-linked steel chains, which had been given plenty of "slack" so that they would "give," to a certain extent, under the initial impact of the assailing Tank. Machine-guns in plenty were behind the barricade; others were showing their snouts through the glazeless windows of the houses, while nearly a thousand picked German troops held the village.

With a dull thud the blunt nose of the Tank encountered the massive obstruction. Ralph had avoided making for the centre of the barricade, and had steered his command towards the right-hand side of the road. The tree-trunks were levered aside under the irresistible pressure of the ponderous mass of moving steel, sand-bags flew in all directions, while the chains, pinned down under the tractor-bands, failed utterly to justify the confidence that the Huns had placed upon them.

Thousands of machine-gun bullets splayed upon the Tank's sides, bombs burst all around her; yet scorning such trivialities the Tank bumped over the debris of the demolished barricade, her guns spitting lead with terrific effect upon the field-grey clad troops.

The first house in the street attracted Setley's attention. Save for a few shell-holes in the walls and that it was roofless the building was otherwise almost intact. From an upper window projected the nozzle of a Flammenwerfer apparatus. Although the weapon was not brought into use against the Tank, Ralph guessed that it was being kept inactive for a purpose. Should the British troops force an entrance into the street, the diabolical contrivance would then be brought to bear upon the dense crowd of khaki-clad Tommies.

Setley's command held on as if with the intention of traversing the village street, until with a sharp turn it bore down upon the house in which the liquid-fire party waited to do their barbarous work.

Striking the front wall obliquely the Tank smashed her way into the building. Stones and bricks were flung asunder, beams began to crash from the upper floors. The Huns, uttering yells of terror, either tumbled headlong upon the roof of the Tank and thence rolled off and were crushed between her sides and the tottering brickwork, or else they clung desperately to the remaining walls and beams. The liquid-fire apparatus fell with the men, the cylinder bursting and discharging its contents all over the Tank and the surrounding debris. Had any of the Boches seized the opportunity and applied a light to the inflammable fluid it would have resulted in Ralph and his men being roasted alive in their steel cage; but, fortunately for them, the disaster did not take place.

It had been Ralph's intention to force his Tank completely through the building, but this task was beyond the powers of the motor-propelled fortress. Vainly the tractor-bands revolved, grinding to powder the brick rubble, yet without gaining another inch.

Failing to forge ahead the Tank endeavoured to back out of the blind alley in which she found herself. With the reversing of her motors the landship jerked back a couple of feet or more and then sank perpendicularly for a distance of seven or eight feet, so that its roof projected only a couple of feet above the level of the street.

For a few seconds the sickening thud knocked the stuffing out of the Tank's crew. Used to bumps and jars though they were they had never before experienced the effect of falling with a hideous thud for a vertical distance of nearly three yards. They were in total darkness, for so dense were the clouds of dust and smoke that the daylight was completely obscured.

When the dust had subsided sufficiently to allow the murky light to penetrate, Ralph took stock of the position. Through the gap in the outer wall that the Tank had made he could see a considerable extent of the village street. Crowds of Germans were rushing up to reinforce the men at the partly demolished barricade, from which Ralph concluded that the British infantry had begun to make the attempt to rush the village.

"If only we had a gun able to bear upon that mob, sir," exclaimed Sergeant Alderhame, "we could enfilade the whole crowd."

It was a vain wish, for in falling the muzzles of the quickfirers had been held up by the brickwork, with the result that they had been wrenched from their mountings, while the mound of rubble was a few inches too high to enable the maxims to be depressed sufficiently to bear upon the Huns in the street.

None of the enemy paid any attention to the stranded Tank. Perhaps the imminent danger of the attacking infantry exercised the prior claim. At any rate, the crew of the landship were passive spectators of the combat, unable to bring a gun to bear upon their foes yet in a position to see most of what was taking place at the commencement of the village street.

Despite machine-gun fire and an incessant fusillade of bombs the storming party gained the gap in the barricade. Two companies of different regiments were the first to get to grips with the enemy. One was a Highland battalion, the other was comprised of men of Ralph's old regiment—the redoubtable Wheatshires.

Both the Jocks and the Tommies were yelling furiously. Amid the babel of voices could be heard the ominous shout of "No Quarter!" The men were up against the Prussian Guard, and there were old scores to pay off. Both the Wheatshires and the Highlanders had cause to remember a certain incident earlier in the war, when under pressure of overwhelming numbers the men had to give ground. Every wounded Briton left on the field was mercilessly bombed or bayoneted, and the perpetrators of this cruel and unnecessary act were Huns of the Prussian Guard. No wonder, then, that it was now a case of te quoque.

Magnificently the khaki-clad men came on. Numbers fell, but

93

still the forward movement was maintained. Up and over they swarmed. Bombs met bombs, bayonet crossed bayonet, rifle-butts descended with sickening thuds on heads. Men badly wounded grappled madly on the ground, regardless of those who trampled on them, their one object being to "do in" their immediate antagonists. Shells from German light field guns were dropping into the pack of friend and foe, till the air rained blood.

In the fury of the fight the combatants were scornful of the dangers. To Ralph, temporarily a mere onlooker, the ghastliness of the whole business was apparent. The hollow mockery of modern civilization stood unmasked. Was it merely to satisfy the insensate craving for glory on the part of that megalomaniac Emperor that millions of Huns and their vassals poured out their blood like water, and more equal numbers of Britons and their Allies freely risked their lives to thwart the sanguinary ambitions of militant Prussianism?

The Kaiser had sown the wind and was now reaping the whirlwind. Whether the present war would be the last, and the sword finally beaten into a ploughshare, still remained to be proved. In calmer moments would the Great Powers grasp the full significance of the devastating and murderous effect of modern war, or is the primeval instinct so deeply rooted in mankind that as long as the world exists international disputes must be settled by the arbitrament of the sword?

The sight of the frenzied mob of hale, active men, most of whom had until a few months before been engaged in eminently peaceful commercial and agricultural pursuits and had been almost entirely ignorant of the use of the rifle, seemed to prove otherwise. Beneath the veneer of civilization the fighting instinct, controlled by centuries of law-governed authority, there still remained the pugnacious instinct. And now, to quote a well-known critic, "the lid of hell was off," with a vengeance.

For a futile ten minutes pandemonium reigned. Mingled with the rattle of machine-guns, the sharp reports of rifle-shots, and the crash of steel, were shouts of vengeful triumph and the cries of the wounded. Through the eddying clouds of dust and smoke tiles and bricks from the shelled houses flew in showers. Occasionally whole buildings would collapse like a pack of cards, burying the German machine gunners in the ruins. Fires, too, were breaking out to add to the horrors of the scene, while with typical indifference the German artillery were dropping shrapnel and gas-shells in the midst of the pack of swaying and struggling combatants.

Beyond the barricade the advance came to a standstill. For a few moments the tide swayed erratically, until the opposing troops were hampered by the dead and wounded. Masses of Germans were hurriedly rushed up through a gap in the otherwise faultless British artillery barrage, and hurled themselves into the fray.

The situation looked critical until a brawny Highlander sprang upon the captured barricade and, holding unsupported a ponderous Lewis gun, pumped in a tray of ammunition over the heads of his comrades. Then, with renewed shouts of "Scotland for Ever!" on the part of the Jocks, and the dogged "Stick it, the Wheatshires!" the British swept forward with an irresistible rush. The majority of the Prussians threw down their arms and fled, to find their retreat cut off by other British battalions, who, assisted by the Tanks, had completed the turning movement. Some of the Huns dashed precipitately to their underground retreats, with parties of British bombers hard at their heels to rout them out of their deep dug-outs.

The fortress village of Néancourt had fallen, but it was a mere incident in the vast field of operations in connection with the Greater Push. Until the Von der Golz Redoubt was in British hands the day's objective could not be considered as achieved.

CHAPTER XIX
THE MINED TUNNEL

"A dozen wellnigh breathless Huns, with greasy uniform and battered equipment, struggling to dive into the cellar in which Ralph's Tank had become a "fixture," roused the crew to action.

The Germans, with their intimate local knowledge, expected to find a safe retreat, until, to their consternation, they were confronted by the blunt nose of the stranded landship and covered by two maxims that could be brought to bear upon them although unable to be trained over the pile of rubble that lay betwixt the Tank and the street.

"Hands up!" shouted Ralph.

The order was obeyed instantly.

"Ye vos Sachsen!" called out an imploring voice. "Mercy, Kamerad."

The statement was a false one, and Setley knew it.

"You are Prussians," he replied; "but we'll give you quarter. Keep your hands up. The first man who lowers his arms will be shot."

Keeping close to the bows of the landship the crowd of now terrified Huns obeyed the instructions. Throwing open the armoured door, Corporal Anderson and two others of the crew emerged from the Tank and deftly removed the prisoners side-arms and ammunition. This done, they stood by to warn any parties of British bombers who in the heat of the pursuit might hurl their devastating missiles into the cellar.

In the midst of his task Anderson spotted one man's hand stealthily approaching his pocket.

"Wot 'ave you got there, old sport?" enquired the corporal, gripping the Hun's wrist. "Search 'im, Smutty," he added, addressing one of the Tommies.

The private did so, and discovered a small automatic pistol.

"So that's the bloomin' game, eh?" enquired Ginger. "Let 'im go, Smutty. Now, look to yourself, Fritz. I'm a-goin' to dot you one."

The German evidently understood, and clenching his fists stood on his guard. The next instant he was flat on his back, contemplating the superb display of a galaxy of stars that danced before his fast-closing eyes.

"What's up, Ginger?" asked Alderhame, and, glancing keenly at one of the prisoners, suddenly lapsed into his unbreakable habit of quoting the bard:

"O world, thy slippery turns. Friends now fast sworn
Unseparable, shall within this hour,
On a dissension of a doit, break out
To bitterest enmity."

To which the prisoner replied, in a faultless English accent:

"Alderhame! I little thought to see you here. Let me see: only three years and six months ago we were on the boards together in Much Ado about Nothing."

"And now," added Alderhame, "we're producing Measure for Measure."

"I hope it will be All's Well that Ends Well," rejoined the German. "I'm properly fed up with this war, and will be glad to be out of it."

"You will be—in a prison camp in England," the sergeant assured him. "We'll see that you are sent under escort to the rear. Unless your own guns cop you there'll be nothing to fear. What made the crowd of you make a dive for this cellar?"

"I don't mind telling you now," he said, in a low voice. "There's a tunnel. That Tank has blocked up the entrance. It communicates with our reserve lines, and the whole place is heavily mined. I would advise you to clear out as soon as possible, for when our people have waited sufficiently long to enable our troops to withdraw—the few that are left, that is—the village will be blown to atoms."

Strong-nerved though he was, the ex-actor felt a cold shiver in the neighbourhood of his spine. The possibility of being in close proximity to a quantity of high explosive that would explode by the act of touching a key—and more than likely a Hun was at that very instant toying with the electric battery that would fire the charge—was enough to make any man blench.

With an effort he pulled himself together.

"All right," he said, addressing his former brother actor and present enemy. "I'll send you out under escort. Yes, the whole crowd of you, I mean."

Obtaining Second-Lieutenant Setley's permission, Alderhame despatched the prisoners under the charge of Corporal Anderson and two men. The moment they had gone Alderhame imparted the grave news to his superior officer.

"Send a man to warn the Divisional Officer of the troops holding the village," ordered Ralph. "We'll have to abandon the Tank, I fancy."

At an order the crew hurriedly prepared to leave the shelter of the stranded landship, but before they could do so a terrific concussion shook the already tottering walls of the cellar, and an avalanche of bricks from the upper part of the walls descended with a crash, completely cutting off their retreat.

"Pleasant," remarked Ralph. "With a mine somewhere under you and H.E. shells dropping overhead, and unable to get out of this hole, life is a bit exciting. No, Alderhame; no more Shakespeare, please. We'll try and find the tunnel to which your German acquaintance referred. By the by, who is he?"

"He was in the same Repertoire Company with me," replied the ex-actor. "It was in those dim and distant days before the war, yet I remember how we parted."

He paused reflectively. Setley looked at him enquiringly.

"Well?" he asked tentatively.

"It was just before Treasury—that is, the weekly pay-day. He borrowed a sovereign—maybe you recollect what that is, or was: a circular flat disc of shining gold, for which one had to display a certain amount of affection. He cleared out shortly afterwards, and I haven't seen that Jimmy o' Goblin since—and don't expect to. However, sir, he's done us a good turn warning us about the mine, though it were to save his own skin."

In the intense gloom the crew of the Tank sought for the

entrance of the tunnel. Cautiously loosening brickwork and removing piles of rubble they at length found the object of their quest—a long, narrow, concreted passage that was originally intended for a communication between the vast subterranean rooms under the village.

"Be careful, sir," cautioned Sergeant Alderhame, as Ralph flashed his electric torch. "There might be some Huns lurking down here."

"Hardly," objected Setley. "It seemed to be common knowledge amongst the Prussians that the place is mined. They'll keep clear. The trouble is, I take it, to discover and disconnect the electric wires before they spring the whole show."

The subaltern and his men hastened down the passage. If ever there was a race against time this was. At eighty paces from the mouth further progress was barred by a formidable barrier of sand-bags—the "tamping" by which the main force of the explosion would be diverted from what would otherwise be the easiest path—an horizontal direction along the tunnel.

"We'll have to shift that lot," said Ralph encouragingly. "All hands together, lads."

It was a tough task, for five yards' thickness of sand-bags had to be removed before the mine chamber was reached. It was a nerve-racking task when the huge store of explosive stood revealed in the glare of an electric torch. At any moment the stuff might explode.

"It'll save the sanitary squad a job if it does," remarked one of the men grimly, "Anyway, it's a mighty quick death—none of that rotten hanging about."

Five minutes later more work resulted in the discovery of two insulated wires that met in a metal box containing the primer. With a sigh of relief Ralph severed the wires. Unless there were more sets the immediate danger was over.

All this time the place was trembling under the concussion of heavy shells overhead. Presently with remarkable suddenness the shelling ceased.

"What does it mean, I wonder?" thought Ralph. "It can't be that our fellows have been compelled to give ground. We must endeavour to get out of this hole and see what's doing."

Bidding the men bring a small quantity of the explosive with them, Setley retraced his way. During his absence more rubble had fallen, and the roof of the Tank was covered with a tightly jammed mass of broken bricks.

"Looks healthy, sir," commented Alderhame.

"Yes," agreed Ralph. "It seems as if we are to stop here until we are dug out, unless we can contrive to blow away this mass of rubble. Unfortunately, I am not expert in the art of the use of explosives."

"There's one of our fellows who used to be a quarryman," announced the sergeant. "I'll get him."

In answer to his call, a little sharp-featured Welshman stepped forward.

"Yes," he replied, in a shrill falsctto. "I have blasted stone for the last three years. I do not know what strength this stuff has, but we'll try."

Taking about seven pounds of the explosive the Welshman rammed it in a cavity in the wall of rubble, filled in the mouth with sand-bags brought from the mine gallery, and laid a fuse of cordite, obtained by opening half a dozen cartridges.

"All ready, sir," he reported. "Get back all of you. I'll fire it. It'll burn for thirty seconds, I guess, and that'll be enough for me to hook it."

The rest of the crew entered the Tank, the door being left open for the brave Welshman to gain shelter before the explosion.

Presently a match flickered in the gloom, followed by the sizzling of the sticks of cordite, which burned with comparative slowness when not under pressure.

With a furious bound the Welshman leapt into the Tank, his head butting into the stomach of a comrade who was holding the door in readiness to slam it the moment the man had gained shelter.

Even in the midst of danger the two began mutual recriminations, the Welshman asking "what the silly idiot meant by getting in his way," the other retorting by requesting him in future to use his eyes to see where he was going.

The argument ended with the terrific roar of the explosion, the sound intensified in the confined space. Fragments of the brickwork rattled on the Tank's armoured snout, clouds of acrid-smelling smoke wafted into the crowded interior of the landship, but the object was achieved.

Opening the door, Ralph saw sunlight filtering through the dust-laden atmosphere. Making his way along the new exit, he cautiously reconnoitred. The street was practically empty, save for the corpses that littered the ground and a group of staff officers who had evidently just emerged from taking cover.

"Confound you, sir!" roared a portly major-general. "What game do you think you're playing? Do you know you nearly blew us sky-high? Confound you, again!"

Setley waited until the irate officer had spoken his mind; then, saluting, made a brief report of his discovery.

"There you are, Richards; I told you so," exclaimed the staff officer, turning to one of his entourage. "The place is mined. Suppose it's safe now?"

"I think so, sir," replied Ralph.

"It may come in handy against the Von der Golz Redoubt, in case our men fail to secure a footing," observed the major addressed as Richards.

"There's no failure about it," snapped the major-general. "Send an orderly to the officer commanding the Royal Engineer detachment and request him to take steps to remove the explosive from the mine chamber. And what were you doing there?" he added, directing his attention to Setley. Evidently an explanation at least was necessary to justify the explosion that had all but settled a group of staff officers.

"Tank, eh? What made you turn her into a cellar? Didn't know? Well, you jolly well ought to. At a time when every available Tank is required in front of the Von der Golz Redoubt you topple the bally thing into a cellar."

Ralph was heartily glad to find himself dismissed from the presence of the peppery staff officer. He felt considerably ill-used. Instead of receiving a word of thanks for his resourcefulness in saving the captured position from being blown to hits, he had been "rapped over the knuckles."

"Here's a pioneer section just arrived, sir," reported Sergeant Alderhame. "If you saw the company commander perhaps he would spare enough men to help us dig a way out. It won't take much work, I think. The rubble has been well sifted by the bursting charge."

The officer readily consented to assist in the salvage operations. After all, the Tank had settled on the floor of the cellar, which was about eight feet below the ground-level. Before she had come to a standstill she had given forward for nearly five yards, and the whole of this space was now filled in with bricks and mortar, forming a fairly steep gradient.

Working strenuously for twenty minutes the fatigue party succeeded in levelling the slope sufficiently to enable the Tank to back. Fortunately, the motors and tractor-bands were intact. The mounting of one of the quickfirers was damaged beyond repair, the other was put in order by the crew.

Amidst the cheers of the men the Tank climbed, stern-

100

foremost, out of her place of imprisonment and gained the shell-pitted street.

An orderly, doubling towards the British lines, stopped by the side of the freed machine.

"Can you push forward, sir?" he asked. "The infantry are being held up. There are only five Tanks left in action."

CHAPTER XX
THE FALL OF THE VON DER GOLZ REDOUBT

"On clearing the other end of the captured village of Néancourt Ralph was able to form a fairly comprehensive idea of the present state of operations.

The Von der Golz Redoubt, one of the strongest positions in the boasted Wotan Line, was still held by the Huns. The British guns were thundering furiously against it. The marvel was that the men could stand such a gruelling, but the Huns did, keeping to the shelter of their deep dug-outs and manning the defences the moment the guns "lifted." Hundreds of Prussians must at that moment be entombed in those dug-outs, of which the entrances had caved in under the terrific power of the H.E. shells, yet hundreds more were available to hold the redoubt "at all costs."

During the lull between the cessation of the bombardment and the numerous but hitherto fruitless infantry assaults British airmen had flown over the redoubt, bombing the defences and even employing machine-gun fire against the tenacious grey-coats. The airmen were in turn attacked by Hun machines, and during the progress of the fighting on land combats in the "vasty air" were taking place unheeded by the grimly contesting troops in and around the Von der Golz Redoubt.

Deftly picking her way betwixt the scores—nay, hundreds—of bodies of dead and wounded that littered the ground, Setley's Tank approached the closely grouped Tommies who, hugging the earth to avoid the ubiquitous machine-guns, were awaiting the order to advance.

Of the other Tanks the tops of three could be discerned showing above a rise in the terrain. Two more had just advanced against the formidable defences, and both had failed gloriously.

"The guns are lifting, sir," reported Sergeant Alderhame.

"Good business!" muttered Ralph. "I'm fed up with this inaction. Another ten minutes will decide whether we are booked or not."

Crunching her way over the shallow trenches held by the British stormers, the Tank floundered through the vast shell-craters that up to a few minutes before had been torn up by the British guns. Quite recently there had been a system of trenches there— those deep, concrete-reinforced, scientifically constructed ones that had taken the Huns months to perfect. Every trace of their earthworks had been obliterated.

Beyond lay a triple line of barbed wire. By one of those freakish circumstances the entanglements had escaped the devastating hail of shells. A few posts had been shattered, some strands of wire cut through, but, generally, this defence work was as efficacious as ever, as the crowd of bodies in khaki and field-grey that were "hung up" on the tenacious barbs testified.

A bomb dropped from a hostile machine fell within ten yards of the Tank. In spite of her bulk and weight, the huge fabric trembled under the concussion.

"Beastly mean trick!" thought Ralph. "That Hun airman knows that we cannot see him, and that we don't carry antis. Wonder what our fliers are doing to let him amuse himself in this manner?"

With a sickening crash a biplane came to earth, right in the path of the moving Tank. A glance at the twisted wreckage showed that the infamous Black Cross was painted on the planes. Ralph had a smart answer to his question. Our airmen had been busy up aloft.

Setley did not trouble to turn aside his command. Right over the debris of the German biplane she waddled, crushing metal and wood into an unrecognizable pulp, and then thrust her blunt nose into the outer line of barbed wire.

Like a rhinoceros tearing up jungle grass with its formidable horns the Tank set about to destroy the entanglements. Posts snapped off like carrots, coils of wire suddenly released from tension quivered in the air until borne down and buried deep in the earth by the broad traction bands of the landship. The while machine-gun bullets rattled harmlessly against her armoured hide, bombs exploded on, against, and underneath the terrible war-machine. The car of Juggernaut would cut a very poor show compared with this motor-propelled fortress.

Other Tanks were engaged in similar operations, keeping parallel to the line of direction of the hostile trenches and methodically uprooting the entanglements in as many minutes as it had taken the Germans days to set up in position. Having completed this part of the programme the Tanks made for the sand-bagged parapet at the raised end of the glacis, while simultaneously with this movement the whistles went, and the British infantry rushed forward with an irresistible élan.

Their attention divided between the terrifying landships, that were crunching over emplacements and trenches, and the glittering array of bayonets, the German machine-gunners, unfortunately for them, did not take into account a couple of British biplanes, Cleaving through the dense eddying clouds of smoke and recklessly disregarding the bursting shells the intrepid airmen descended to within a hundred feet of the Von der Golz Redoubt and the adjacent trenches. A hail of bullets from the airmen's Lewis guns—death-dealing hornets—caught the Huns unawares, creating havoc in the dense masses of grey-coated infantry.

Poison gas shells added to the horror of the desperate struggle. Aerial torpedoes, missiles from trench mortars, and the deadly shells from the Stokes' guns, rained upon the enemy position. It was a wonder that the Huns stood it as they did; yet, with their back to the wall and unable to retreat or even to take shelter in their deep dug-outs, they fought with a courage that could only be described as fanatical.

Ploughing her way through the mazes of barbed wire Setley's Tank came astride a deep trench that flanked one side of the redoubt to where the glacis terminated in what was a few hours before an elaborately constructed covered way bristling with loopholes, each one of which showed the muzzle of a machine-gun. Now there was little left but a crumbling mound of earth and disrupted sand-bags, in which half-buried Germans still maintained a furious but erratic rifle-fire.

Almost before he was aware of it Ralph found himself within the once considered impregnable redoubt. There was practically nothing to mark its position. It was only when he found himself confronted by a landship strongly resembling his own that he realized that he had gained his objective, for the oncoming Tank was not, as he at first imagined, one of German workmanship, but a British machine that had entered the redoubt on the opposite side.

Narrower and narrower grew the encircling ring of khaki. With bomb and bayonet the British infantry swept the flattened earthwork, until the surviving Huns, finding further resistance useless, threw down their arms and raised shouts of "Kamerad." Greatly to their surprise they found that, contrary to the statements of their officers, the British Tommy is a generous victor. As if by magic the heat of combat gave place to a light-hearted, almost considerate, treatment of the remnant of the garrison of the redoubt, and it was by no means an uncommon sight to see a British soldier bind up the wounds he had inflicted on a German only a few minutes previously.

The paucity of prisoners testified to the stubbornness of the enemy resistance. Quickly the captives were formed up and marched to the advance cages—a task not without great peril, since the German gunners, according to their customary indifference to their ill-fated comrades, were putting up a barrage behind the captured position.

With the clearing of the remnants of the garrison the victorious Tommies began to put the shell-tortured ground into a state of defence. They were now well astride the vaunted Hindenburg Line, and it was pretty certain that the Huns would make a strong and determined counter-attack in order to attempt to wrest the position from the victors. The attack would be soon— before the British heavy guns could be moved forward, and already the railway corps were placing sections of rails in position to enable the twelve- and fourteen-inch monsters to be sent forward. Once they were in position the Von der Golz was lost for good and all to the Huns, and they knew it.

There was no rest for the Tanks that had escaped being placed hors de combat. Orders were given for the landships to push ahead and hold the counter-attacking force in check.

"Independent action, you know," remarked the commanding officer of the Landship Section. "So out you go, and the very best of luck."

Ralph knew what that meant. It was one of the most hazardous enterprises that a Tank could be called upon to perform. With a quickening of his pulses he gave the word for the motors to be started once more and steered his armoured mobile fortress in the direction of the unknown territory that for the last two years or more had been firmly held by the Huns.

"By Jove! Alderhame," he exclaimed, "we're on a big thing this time. Wouldn't miss it for worlds."

"Let's hope we won't," added Sergeant Alderhame grimly. "The present world is quite good enough for me for a long time to come, Boches notwithstanding."

CHAPTER XXI
TRAPPED

"""'Old 'ard, chapses; 'old 'ard!"

"What's that?" enquired Ralph, hearing a voice but unable to distinguish the words owing to the din both within and without.

"It's Corporal Anderson, sir," reported one of the crew.

Setley gave orders for the door to be opcncd. With the Tank still in motion, George Anderson clambered into the interior and gave vent to an exclamation of profound relief.

"Thoughter wasn't goin' to pick you up, sir," he remarked. "I got them Boches back all right, and then blow me if I could find you anywheres. If I've chased one bloomin' Tank I've chased a dozen, to say nothin' of a few cripples, although I didn't think as 'ow anythink could 'appen to this 'ere gadget."

The corporal was too modest to relate the peculiar adventures he had undergone in his finally successful quest; how he had twice been knocked flat by exploding shells, and how he had alighted upon a "pocket" of armed Germans who had been overlooked in the forward movement. With his utmost coolness Ginger had beckoned to a totally imaginary crowd of Tommies, and at the same time had shouted to the Huns to "'Ands up," with the result that more time was taken up in the return journey to the advance cages, shepherding eleven Guardsmen in front of him.

"Have you seen anything of Mr. Danvers?" enquired Ralph.

"Yes, sir," replied Ginger. "It was 'im wot told me where you was. 'Is Tank was just off along the Hoppy Road, goin' like a young racehorse."

It was in the direction of the fortified village of Oppy that Ralph was making. At this point the massing of German infantry had been reported by aerial scouts. By road and rail reserves had been rushed up from other sections of the Hindenburg Line. The Tanks were to cut the enemy's communications, if possible, and hinder the concentration of Germans for the counter-attack.

The shell-pitted ground over which Setley's Tank nosed her way was no longer under fire. The enormous craters had been torn up by the bombardment of the British heavies. The guns were now being pushed forward, and although the German artillery was still putting up a strong barrage the projectiles were falling between the captured Von der Golz Redoubt and Néancourt village.

Every foot of the way was strewn with evidences of the devastating effect of the pounding of the shells. Numerous corpses, half-buried limbers, dismounted field-guns, and a medley of shattered transport waggons testified to the terrible gruelling the Huns had received behind their trenches. Here and there were heaps of brickwork mingled with still smouldering woodwork—all that was left of a dozen villages. Hardly a tree was left standing. The few that were had been stripped of branches and reared their scorched and seared trunks like grim gallows trees silhouetted against the black and yellow waste of smoke.

Already British cavalry were patrolling considerably beyond the ground held by the infantry. The men, filled with wild enthusiasm at being able to be in the saddle and after their foes, were making short work of all small detachments of Germans who had got out of touch with the main body.

For three miles Setley's Tank pursued her way before losing sight of the cavalry. Occasionally a Hun sniper would send a bullet pinging harmlessly against her steel sides, but the crew loftily ignored the useless compliment. With bigger game in view, the individual German marksman could be simply left alone.

As the Tank approached a ruined wall a khaki-clad figure appeared as from the earth and began running towards the oncoming machine, waving his hands in a manner that clearly indicated his wish for the landship to stop.

"He's an officer, sir," reported Sergeant Alderhame. "Wonder what he's doing so far ahead? Prisoner, perhaps, who has managed to give the Huns the slip."

Giving orders for the motors to be switched off, Ralph brought the Tank to a dead stop, and unbolting the armoured door awaited the officer's approach. Caution urged him not to throw the door wide open, in case there were snipers about, but without drawing the fire of a single rifle the stranger gained the Tank and at Ralph's invitation nimbly hopped in.

"Glad to have fallen in with you," was the new-comer's greeting. He was a tall sparely built man in the uniform of a captain of the Royal Flying Corps. "My name is Cludderborough. I suppose I have already been reported as missing. I was brought down a week ago last Friday. Nearly came a good old crash, but got off lightly, with the exception of a sprained ankle. I managed to escape during the bending of the Hindenburg Line. That was early this morning. So far I've not done so badly, but my ankle is giving me a lot of pain. So that is why I signalled for you to stop."

"But we aren't going your way," remarked Ralph. "We're off on a sort of independent cruise, don't you know. I would suggest that you enjoy the hospitality of the nearest shell-hole until our cavalry patrols come up. They are not so very far behind."

Captain Cludderborough did not hail the proposition with enthusiasm. In fact, he promptly "turned it down."

"Too jolly risky," he observed. "Already snipers have put shots through my coat. You have no objection to taking me as a passenger, I hope? I may come in pretty useful, since I know the country behind the German line very well, both from the standpoint of an aerial observer and from that of an escaped prisoner."

Ralph did not immediately accept the offer. There was no good reason why he should not do so. Rapidly weighing up the situation, he decided that no great harm could be done in the giving the Flying Corps officer a "lift."

"I must warn you," he said, "that we are about to engage in a particularly hazardous enterprise. If you are anxious to rejoin your Corps as quickly as possible I should advise you to accept my proposition. If, on the other hand, you think you can materially assist us then by all means come along."

"Right," rejoined the captain promptly. "You are about to cut the Germans' lines of communication in the neighbourhood of Oppy? There's a beautiful temporary trestle-bridge which the Huns have recently made to take the place of a steel viaduct brought down by one of our airmen. This Tank ought to crumple the structure as easily as if it were a pack of cards. By the by, have you a snack of something to offer me? I am absolutely ravenous."

"Get Captain Cludderborough something to eat, Corporal Anderson," said Ralph. "You'll have to excuse our lack of courtesy," he added. "The limited space, the jolting motion, and above all the fact that we are in an hostile country, prevents me from doing the honours properly."

"Where's your map?" asked the captain, after he had finished his meal. "Ah, there you are: no sign of the viaduct is shown. The thing's beastly inaccurate. See that slight river almost ahead? That's Nôtre Dame d'Huy. The railway line skirts the other side of the hill. There's a fairly broad valley between Nôtre Dame and the hill on the right. Both eminences are crossed with trenches, but they are not held. The Huns were clearing out as I slipped through. It's my belief that they have purposely retired in order to leave a tempting gap for our troops, and then they'll start shelling from both sides. However, it's too early for that, so we ought to get through and astride the railway line before they spot us."

Captain Cludderborough spoke with such decision that his words carried conviction. With his aid there was certainly a good chance of pulling off a highly successful coup. By destroying the railway bridge the transference of German troops from the southern sectors of the line to the threatened regions would be seriously impeded. By the time the men were taken by a circuitous loop-line the British heavy guns would be in position ready to meet the expected counter-attack upon the village of Néancourt and the captured Von der Golz Redoubt.

Steadily the Tank approached the gap between the two hills. So far all went well. Captain Cludderborough's statement that the Germans had abandoned the rising ground was evidently confirmed, for there were no signs of any living Huns.

"Rummy sort of show, sir," commented Sergeant Alderhame, as the defence came in sight. "I should feel inclined to go smack bang over the hill instead of through that gap."

"Eh?" interrupted the captain. "You would, would you? Not only would you have to surmount difficult ground, but you would be absolutely on the sky-line and a target for every German quickfirer within ten thousand yards."

"Very good, sir," said the sergeant quietly. Having made his protest, he had done all he could in that direction. He was bound to obey unquestionably the decision of his superior officer, and since Setley agreed to the captain's remark the matter was settled.

Nevertheless, Sergeant Alderhame's words impressed themselves upon Ralph's mind The subaltern decided that he would be unfeignedly glad when the Tank emerged from that forbidding valley. The very stillness, contrasting vividly with the rumble of the distant guns, seemed out of place.

The defile was nearly three quarters of a mile in length, its width averaging only a hundred yards. On either side the ground rose with tolerable abruptness, the height of the encircling hills being considerably greater than it had appeared when viewed from a distance. Half-way to the summit a triple line of trenches encompassed both hills, but these were as silent as the tents of Sennacherib when the angel of death had passed through the Assyrian hosts.

"Nearly through," remarked Captain Cludderborough, who had taken his stand at Ralph's elbow. "You'll see the precious trestle-bridge in half a shake."

As he spoke there was a loud roar. A dense cloud of smoke and dust leapt skywards at the distance of a furlong in front of the Tank. Almost simultaneously another explosion occurred at a similar distance to the rear. The Huns had sprung two land mines. The Tank, caught betwixt them, was trapped, and to impress the fact more strongly upon her hundreds of Germans appeared from the hitherto apparently deserted trenches.

The cold muzzle of an automatic pistol was pressed against Ralph's temple and the mocking voice of the pseudo Captain Cludderborough remarked:

"You will do well, sir, to order your men to surrender instantly. There is no escape. Give in without resistance and you will be accorded honourable treatment. I, Kapitan Karl von Hoerfelich, guarantee it."

Von Hoerfelich was a resourceful German who, attracted by the offer of a large monetary reward for the capture of an intact British Tank, and animated by a strong desire to further the interest of the Imperial arms, had employed a daring ruse in order to attempt to achieve his object. Speaking English with the utmost fluency and having a thorough knowledge of British military matters—a knowledge gained by a seven years' exile in Great Britain, during which time he had taken up a menial position as a waiter at a famous Army Club—he submitted his plan to his superiors.

In brief, he was to personate a British airman who had made a forced landing behind the German lines. The chance of meeting with a Tank operating far in advance of the infantry was realized, and so far he had successfully lured the landship into a formidable ambush. The moment had come for him boldly to proclaim his identity, his firm belief being that seeing the uselessness of resistance, the crew would tamely surrender at his summons.

Completely taken aback when he felt the muzzle of the pistol against his temple, Second-Lieutenant Setley wisely refrained from obeying his natural inclination of grappling with his declared enemy.

"Wouldn't it be advisable to stop the motors?" asked Ralph coolly. "We'll come an awful crash in that beastly hole ahead if we don't. It looks quite fifty feet deep, doesn't it?"

Deceived by the apparent simplicity and urgency of the question, von Hoerfelich gave a brief glance through the slit in the armour in order to verify Setley's statement.

Quick as was his action, Ralph was quicker. With a sharp upward movement of his elbow he jerked the German's automatic pistol. At the same time he ducked his head and gripped the Hun round the waist. Interlocked in a grim embrace, the two men struggled in the confined space while the Tank ambled uncontrolled towards the yawning mine-crater.

Something hard grazed Ralph's cheek and struck the German

on the point of his chin with a dull hideous thud. With a muttered "Wot's yer game, old sport?" Ginger Anderson had planted a terrific left-hander on a vulnerable part of the Boche's anatomy. The fellow's resistance collapsed, and he dropped inertly at the little corporal's feet.

Recovering his disturbed senses, Ralph shouted to the men to open fire; then turning the Tank in as small a curve as possible he steered the monster up the steep side of the ravine, where hundreds of the enemy, assisted by the natural defence of the ground, awaited with complete confidence the capture of the trapped Tank.

CHAPTER XXII
TANK VERSUS LOCOMOTIVE

"The tactics of the landship that, according to their belief, was as good as captured, puzzled the Germans considerably. They waited, expecting to be hailed by the Prussian captain, whom they knew was inside the Tank.

The Huns were quickly undeceived. A withering fire from the Tank's machine-guns catching them unawares played havoc with the soldiers who had rashly left their shelter trenches. At the same time, the landship, heeling over until she appeared to be on the point of capsizing, lumbered bravely up the steeply shelving side of the valley.

The ground, though rocky and irregular, afforded a good grip to the tractor-bands. Small and medium sized boulders she crushed into the softer soil, the larger ones she pushed aside. Brushwood and saplings were rent, the few stunted pine trees in her course were simply uprooted.

"By Jove!" ejaculated Setley delightedly. "She's doing it. I was rather doubtful whether she would tackle that gradient. Now, you bounders, how's that?"

The Tank was astride the first trench—a deep and narrow excavation, but, unlike those on flat ground, following the contour of the hillside in a fairly straight line. With her nose resting on the parados and her tractor-bands scooping up sand-bags like a dog scratching at the mouth of a rabbit-hole the landship remained practically stationary for nearly a minute, the maxims each letting loose the best part of a belt of ammunition.

Fortunately there were no field-guns in this section. The

Huns, recovering from their surprise, were, however, letting fly with machine-guns, rifles and bombs, all of which had no appreciable effect upon the armoured mastodon.

The Tank was nearly the cause of her own destruction by remaining astride the trench, for some of the maxim bullets striking a can of detonating powder that had been left over from the amount required to charge the landmines went off with a roar that completely dominated the rattle of musketry.

In spite of her weight and bulk the landship reeled under the terrific blast. Huge rocks were hurled against her sides. When the smoke had cleared away Ralph could form a hasty idea of the nature of the damage. Where the trench had been was a huge semi-crater nearly fifty yards in length. A large portion of the hillside had been blown away, forming an almost perpendicular semicircular cliff. The corresponding half of the circle of displaced earth had crashed into the valley—a vast jumble of rocks, stones, earth and sand-bags, mingled with the corpses of a hundred Germans. And within her own length of the newly formed precipice the Tank rocked on the unstable soil. It was touch-and-go whether she would slither, like a side-slipping motor-car, into the abyss.

Once more mechanical ingenuity triumphed over the forces of nature. Resisting the attraction of gravity and overcoming the tendency to slip on the crumbling, moving soil, the Tank drew steadily away from the danger zone, until gaining firm ground she resumed her upward climb and approached the second line of trenches.

Not a shot came from this part of the defences. The Huns, bewildered and demoralized by the nerve-racking catastrophe and the sight of their comrades being hurled like stones from a catapult, had fled. Even their officers made no effort to keep them back. Not knowing the cause of the explosion they had formed the erroneous idea that the British landship possessed some terrific and hitherto unknown means of destruction and had used it with annihilating results upon the men in the first trench.

"We're through," ejaculated Alderhame. "'Ware the summit, sir; that skunk of a Hun evidently spoke the truth for once in his life when he said we would be shelled if we showed up on the skyline."

"I will," replied Ralph. "I had forgotten. Suppose it was in the excitement of the minute. Any casualties?"

"Private Saunderson has got a gash over the left eye, sir," reported the sergeant. "A splinter of steel must have come in through the sighting aperture. It's not at all a serious wound."

Skirting the rounded top of the hill of Nôtre Dame Ralph

brought his command in sight of the undulating country beyond, an expanse of fertile land dotted with numerous valleys, all of which were fated to be destroyed by the retreating enemy within the next few days. Right in the foreground was the railway line, the viaduct being less than half a mile from the moving Tank. Detached parties of Germans and isolated individuals were hurrying away from the approaching British troops, who were now at least three miles off.

In the distance a column of white vapour stood out clearly against the clouds of black and brown smoke and announced the fact that a train was on the move, making in a north-westerly direction. It was one of many bringing up the German reserves to launch their formidable counter-attack upon the men who had broken Hindenburg's line.

"Whack her up for all she's worth," ordered Ralph, addressing the motor mechanic. "Now, lads, it's a race. It's up to us to get to that viaduct before the train can cross."

The bridge, although not marked on Ralph's military map, was in the position indicated by the impersonator of Captain Cludderborough. It crossed a small stream at a point one hundred yards or thereabouts to the north of the original structure that had been bombed and demolished by British airmen. The temporary viaduct was made of huge baulks of timber supporting a central span of only thirty feet. The banks of the stream that flowed underneath were low, the ground sloping gently on the near side but rising with considerable abruptness on the remote side.

With a succession of jolts and bumps the Tank plunged downhill at a greater rate than she had ever done before in her brief yet strenuously exciting career; but notwithstanding the hot pace Setley was forced to come to the conclusion that the troop train would be the first to reach the bridge.

He thought hard. The time for decisive action, bordering on self-sacrifice, was at hand. Unable to destroy the bridge before the train rumbled across he decided to try conclusions with the locomotive.

"Pass the word that any man who wishes may get out," he said to Sergeant Alderhame. "I'm going to ram that engine."

Alderhame bellowed out his superior officer's permission. It would be a comparatively easy matter for the men to alight from the moving Tank, but one and all elected to take their chances with their youthful officer.

Gripping the nearest object that formed a likely hold the men awaited with grim faces and tightly closed lips the impact with an equal target of metal moving at five or six times the rate of the landship.

The driver of the locomotive had spotted the Tank. To Ralph's satisfaction he saw that the German was applying his brakes and shutting off steam. Had he maintained his speed there was a chance that he might have escaped a collision. By easing down he not only played into the hands of his enemy but mitigated the chance of the Tank's destruction.

Had there been time Ralph would have merely steered his Tank across the lines, in which case the weight of the landship would have twisted the track and caused the train to leave the metals. But there was not. To attempt to do so would result in the engine striking the Tank fairly on her side.

Meeting at an aggregate rate of nearly thirty miles an hour the Tank's nose struck the locomotive a glancing blow somewhere in the region of the driver's cab. With a terrific rending of metal and the hiss of escaping steam the engine toppled over on its side, while the carriages either telescoped or lurched over the slight embankment.

As for the Tank, she began to climb upon the wreckage of the vanquished; then turning began to describe a small circle.

It was some minutes before the bruised and shaken crew could realize what had occurred. The tractor-bands on the right-hand side had been shattered by the impact, the left-hand one was intact and still moving. Like a bird wounded in one wing the landship was unable to keep a straight course and could only crawl round and round almost on her own axis.

Although crippled the Tank still retained certain of her powers of offence. Her maxims were trained upon the swarm of dazed and shaken Huns who were emerging from the wrecked carriages. There was no need to open fire. The Germans had a wholesome dread of British landships, a fear based solely upon hearsay since none of these had previously seen a Tank. With upraised hands and cries of "Mercy, Kamerad!" the majority now approached the now motionless landship. The remaining survivors of the collision were either hiding behind the overturned carriages or else scurrying across the fields, in order to put a safe distance between them and the frightful engine of warfare.

"What's to be done with this crush?" enquired Ralph. "We can't fire on the blighters, we can't take them prisoners."

"And if we let them go they'll soon tell their pals, sir," added Alderhame. "The best thing, I take it, is to hold them under the cover of our guns and await events. Our cavalry patrols may be here shortly."

Setley shook his head.

"Won't do," he objected. "More than likely the limits of to-day's gains are already fixed, in which case we may have to wait until next week. I'll order the Boches to clear out. It will leave us free for another task; after that we must take our chances."

The Huns obeyed Ralph's peremptory order with evident hesitation Some of them, perhaps, wanted to be taken prisoners. Fresh from the Russian front they dreaded the horrors of the Ypres salient and the regions of the Somme and Ancre. Others were under the impression that the order to clear out was merely a ruse on the part of the Tank and that directly they were at a certain distance from the latter they would be shot down by her machine-guns.

"Now," declared Ralph, as the handful of Britons were left alone with the dead and dying victims of the deliberate collision. "A couple of men, with a charge of explosive and a two-minute fuse: we're going to settle the bridge."

CHAPTER XXIII
THE LAST STAND

"Refusing Sergeant Alderhame's offer to accompany him and leaving him in charge, Ralph, with Corporal Anderson and a private, emerged from the Tank.

There was no time to be lost. Already Setley had caught sight of a battery of German fixed field guns moving somewhat in the direction of the crippled Tank. Even if the survivors of the troop train did not inform the artillery officers of the presence of the British landship there was not the faintest chance of the huge, multi-coloured target escaping the notice of the gunners.

Bearing the explosive the subaltern and the two men raced to the bridge. Waist deep in water Ginger Anderson placed the charge in a space between the baulks of timber forming one of the principal piers, applied and lit the fuse.

The three started to run back to the shelter of the Tank when the sharp crack of a rifle rang out and Corporal Anderson pitched headlong on his face and rolled over on his back.

"'Ard lines," he gasped. "Properly plugged, an' no chance of gettin' back to Blighty. 'Op it, sir, an' don't worry arter me."

Ralph knelt by the side of his wounded corporal and one-time fellow-private. The other man also stopped and threw himself upon the ground. The time-limit of the fuse was nearly up.

"Where are you hit?" asked Setley.

"Left leg, sir," replied Ginger Anderson.

"No more bloomin' football for me, worse luck. It's like this, sir——"

A deafening crash denoted the fact that the charge had exploded. When the dust cleared away the greater portion of the bridge was no longer in existence. That part of the business had been successfully accomplished.

"Put your hands round my neck and hang on," ordered Setley. "I'm going to carry you in."

With the assistance of the private Anderson was hoisted on the subaltern's back and the last stage of the return journey began, but before Ralph had taken a dozen steps something like a hot-iron seared his shoulder. In spite of the weight of his burden he turned round twice and then collapsed, losing consciousness to the rattle of one of the Tank's machine-guns.

At the report of the rifle-shot that had brought Ginger Anderson down Sergeant Alderhame, keenly on the alert, kept a sharp look-out for the sniper's position. When the second report rang out the sergeant let rip with the machine-gun, with the result that he had the satisfaction of seeing a Hun scurrying for more efficient cover and being brought down as he ran.

A rescue party quickly brought the wounded officer and corporal back to the Tank.

"Bringin' 'em in, sergeant?" asked one of the men. "We're all best outside, I'm thinking. They're bringing up the guns."

"By Jove, so they are!" exclaimed Alderhame. "Yes, outside every man jack of you. We'll be having fifteen-pounder shells this way in half a jiffey."

The operation of abandoning the landship was proceeded with. Sergeant Alderhame was the last man to leave, having previously lit a fuse that would lead to the complete destruction of the Tank. She had played her part nobly, and her reward was destruction at the hands of her crew.

Presently Ralph opened his eyes, to find himself being carried by four of his men. Others were bearing the wounded corporal, while more were carrying off one of the maxims. At the same moment the first of the German shells burst a hundred yards to the rear and within a few feet of the already doomed landship.

"Where are you making for, sergeant?" asked Ralph.

"For that farmhouse, sir," replied Alderhame.

"Better not," protested the wounded subaltern, as resolutely as his bodily weakness permitted. "They'll mark us down for a dead cert if we take up our position there. Select a spot at least two hundred yards away."

The crew of the Tank proceeded on their quest for shelter. Instinctively they realized that they were in a very tight corner, isolated on hostile ground. Nothing short of a miracle, they decided, could extricate them from their dangerous position; yet with unfailing resolution they made up their minds to "fight it out." Death with their faces to the foe was infinitely preferable to the horrors of the life of a prisoner of war in the hands of the Huns.

Keeping to the scanty cover afforded by a slight dip in the ground the dauntless men made their way with the utmost caution. Just as they gained the spot indicated by the officer a crash, completely outvoicing the bursting of the shells, announced that Setley's Tank was no longer in existence.

Propped against a shattered tree-trunk Ralph directed operations for defence, while one of his men attended to his wound.

"Where's the German officer?" he asked suddenly.

Ginger Anderson, who was lying close to his disabled officer, grinned broadly, despite the agony caused by his badly fractured leg.

"I 'it 'im a little too 'ard, sir," he explained. "Meant ter put 'im to sleep in the best perfessional manner, but——"

"He was as dead as a doornail before you left to destroy the bridge, sir," reported Sergeant Alderhame. "We didn't worry to bring his carcase away, and I guess it will be a warning to his pals when they find him. Hullo, sir! You're right. Fritz has started to shell the farmhouse."

Evidently under the impression that the men from the Tank had sheltered in the building the Huns began shelling the conspicuous target. At the third round the place collapsed like a pack of cards.

"If they let it go at that we may even yet have a chance," thought Ralph.

Ten minutes later Alderhame reported a considerable body of Germans coming in the direction of the demolished house, while at the same time the presence of a strong force of hostile infantry was seen between the Tank's crew and the British front.

"No chance of slipping through," decided the sergeant. "We'll lie close and trust to luck. They may not spot us. If they get too curious we'll give them something to remember."

The Germans, on arriving at the site of the farm buildings,

carefully examined the debris. Disappointed in their expectations of finding the bodies of their foes they signalled to the main force. The receipt of this intelligence was followed by an encircling movement, two battalions working round to the right, one to the left, while a regiment of Jagers in extended order advanced immediately on their front.

"They're mighty keen on getting us," said Ralph. "A couple of thousand men at the very least."

About fifty of the Huns who had made their way to the farmhouse were now heading directly for the spot where the British soldiers lay in their scanty cover. It was impossible to escape detection.

"Stand by," whispered Alderhame tersely. He had taken over the command, since Setley was too weak to direct operations effectively.

A guttural shout from one of the leading Germans proclaimed the fact that he had spotted the group of khaki-clad men. A regular fusillade was the immediate outcome of his discovery; but, with the usual indifferent marksmanship of the Hun, the shots flew either wide or else too high.

The maxim, aided by rifle fire, gave the enemy a very unpleasant surprise, and before the first belt of ammunition was exhausted the Germans were bolting for cover.

"Now for a good old shelling," thought Ralph.

But he was mistaken. For some unexplained reason the German field guns had limbered up. Perhaps their presence was urgently required at another point. Instead, the swarm of infantry began to converge upon the isolated handful of Britons, until the position was surrounded by a dense mass of field grey-clad troops.

Even then the Huns forbore to close. Sharpshooters crept forward, taking admirable cover, but, generally speaking, the enemy kept beyond effective rifle distance.

"They're going to wait until its dark and then rush us," decided Alderhame. "By Jove, I never before played to such a crowded audience as this!"

Slowly the time dragged on. Bullets from the skirmishers buzzed incessantly over the defenders' heads. The crew of the Tank replied leisurely, hardly ever throwing away a shot. The maxim was silent. It was no use wasting ammunition on individual foes.

With disconcerting persistence, despite their losses, the Jagers drew nearer and nearer. Numbers of them concentrated in a hollow within eighty yards of the defenders' position, where, immune from fire, they prepared to rush the little band at the point of the bayonet, aided by the use of bombs.

Suddenly disorder appeared in the hostile ranks. Men, bolting for cover, fled for dear life, many of them dropping from a fire more intense than that of Setley's party.

The reason was soon apparent. Waddling over the undulating ground was a British Tank. Spitting out fire as she advanced the rescuing landship made straight for the place where the crew of her destroyed consort held their own, and, taking up a position so as to form a screen from the Germans' fire, she came to a stop.

"Buck up, Setley!" exclaimed Danvers. "Don't keep us waiting. Here's plenty of room inside."

But Setley was temporarily beyond the "bucking up" stage. He had fainted again.

When he recovered consciousness Ralph was in a base hospital. Almost the first question he asked was whether his men were safe. Receiving an affirmative reply, he enquired whether the nature of his wounds would put him out of the running for active service.

"Bless my soul, no!" replied the doctor. "A few months at home and you'll be as fit as a fiddle. Let me be the first to congratulate you, Mr. Setley."

"On what?" asked Ralph.

"Promotion and the D.S.O.," replied the medico. "Both well earned, let me say. Now, don't get excited, or you'll put yourself back. The sooner you get fit the sooner you'll be given the command of one of the latest super-Tanks. I know that for a fact."

"That's good," murmured the wounded lieutenant. "All I hope is that when the Greatest Push comes off I'll again be to the Fore with the Tanks!"